A LOT LIKE CHRISTMAS

A SMALL TOWN SOUTHERN ROMANCE

KAIT NOLAN

A LETTER TO READERS

Dear Reader,

This book is set in the Deep South. As such, it contains a great deal of colorful, colloquial, and occasionally grammatically incorrect language. This is a deliberate choice on my part as an author to most accurately represent the region where I have lived my entire life. This book also contains swearing and pre-marital sex between the lead couple, as those things are part of the realistic lives of characters of this generation, and of many of my readers.

If any of these things are not your cup of

tea, please consider that you may not be the right audience for this book. There are scores of other books out there that are written with you in mind. In fact, I've got a list of some of my favorite authors who write on the sweeter side on my website at https://kaitnolan.com/on-the-sweeter-side/

If you choose to stick with me, I hope you enjoy!

Happy reading!

Kait

CHAPTER 1

"Sugar, are you tying *utensils* on that Christmas tree?"

Undeterred by the *Girl, you crazy* tone, Hannah Wheeler finished attaching the dessert fork to a branch with a short piece of jute and glanced over her shoulder at Omar Buckley, official master of the kitchens at Dinner Belles Diner. Taking advantage of the mid-afternoon lull, he leaned against the counter and watched her with undisguised bafflement.

"You can't judge until I'm done. Trust me." By the time she finished with the tree, the whole thing would be cute, kitchy, and scream "diner." It was just the first phase in her holiday plan to introduce Wishful to the skills she had besides carting trays and taking orders. The phase that would hopefully prove to them—and to herself—that she had the chops to pursue the rest of her revised dream.

Janelle Duncan, the other waitress on duty, who was a lot more interested in checking out Omar and his former running back's body than in Hannah's efforts at decorating, sidled over to him with a conspiratorial head shake. "If we ever run out of flypaper, we can always use that tree. It's at least twice as tacky. Bless her heart."

The lack of cheerleading didn't concern Hannah overmuch. In her previous life, she'd had far more difficult clients to please, and she'd always come through in the end. People usually didn't have any vision until someone showed it to them. And that was fine. She had enough vision for all of them.

Grabbing a spoon and more jute, she turned back to the tree and jolted. A man stood on the other side of the window, peering inside. Hannah could hardly see his eyes past the scruff of a beard and the oily, matted hair. His shoulders hunched against the unseasonably cold weather, and no wonder. The thin denim jacket —worn and stained—was hardly sufficient for the early December temperatures. Seeing the Army green duffle over his shoulder, her heart softened. She had a particular weakness for down-on-their-luck veterans. Offering a friendly smile, she waved for him to come inside.

He blinked at her, expression unchanging, still standing there with a totally unnatural stillness that said he'd been a soldier. Hannah pointed at him and mimed drinking from a cup of coffee. She hoped he took it for the invitation it was and not as some kind of pity. Amping up the smile, she waited. She'd yet to meet the man who could turn away from that smile. Certainly, it had worked to keep her daddy wrapped around her little finger from the time she was knee high.

The stranger was no exception. He strode to the door and came inside, stopping just inside the threshold and scanning the room. She was pretty sure in a matter of seconds he'd cataloged all the exits; had noted her, Omar, and Janelle, as well as the two other patrons; and probably knew where any weapons were likely to be. Or maybe she'd just watched the Bourne movies too many times.

Hannah rose from her crouch beside the tree and held out a hand in welcome. "Please, have a seat. Warm up." Taking a few steps closer to gesture toward the corner booth that had the best visibility in the place, she noted the powerful smell of unwashed body.

He must be homeless. Bless his heart. Hannah had seen that often enough when she'd lived in Atlanta, but here in Wishful, it was all but unheard of. Keeping the smile firmly in place as he sat, back to the wall, she asked, "What can I get you?"

"Just coffee," he rasped in a voice that sounded rusty with disuse.

"Coming right up." With practiced efficiency, Hannah retrieved the coffee pot and turned over the waiting ceramic mug at the table, filling it just high enough that there was room to doctor it, though guy like him would probably drink it black.

He grunted something that sounded like "Thanks" and wrapped his hands around the mug. The skin of his knuckles was chapped with cold.

"Can I interest you in some pie? Mama Pearl makes the best pie in six counties. The pecan in particular is to die for." She leaned in conspiratorially. "But, really, the coconut cream is my favorite."

His gaze slid over to the pie rack on the counter before he shook his head.

She didn't let the smile slip. "Okay then. You just let me know if you need anything."

Replacing the coffee pot, she circled around the counter and into the kitchen, where Omar had resumed his post at the grill. "Be a doll and dish up one of the specials."

"Didn't hear him order the special."

"He didn't. I'm giving it to him anyway. It can come out of my tips."

He gave her an indulgent smile. "Whatever you say, Marshmallow."

Janelle peered through the kitchen window toward his table and kept her voice low. "You sure you want to do anything to encourage him to stay? What if he's not right in the head?"

"Don't be ridiculous," Hannah snapped, gesturing toward Omar. "That's like making the assumption that Omar is a thug because he wears a do rag and likes rap music. It's not only rude, it shows an exceptional lack of compassion." She snatched up the bowl of loaded potato soup so fast the garlic bread stick flew off the plate and onto the stainless-steel counter. Blowing out a breath, Hannah carefully replaced the bread and pushed back out front, working to readjust her expression as she went. Sometimes people just killed her with their ignorance.

The stranger's brows drew together as she

slid the bowl in front of him. "I didn't order this."

She just smiled. "I know. But you look frozen through, so I figured you could use it. On me. And thank you for your service."

The frown was just about the only part of his expression visible as he stared at her. Her smile faltered. Was he offended? She ran through possible apologies in her head, but before she could speak, he nodded in thanks and picked up a spoon.

She left him to his meal, making a quick circuit to check on the other two customers before returning to her decorating. He'd dug into his soup with gusto by then. As she continued tying silverware to the pre-lit tree, she wondered what his story was. He definitely had *Don't Pry* blinking in neon above his head. Was he passing through? Wishful wasn't exactly on the way to anywhere.

She made a fresh pass to top off his coffee, pleased to note the bowl of soup had all but been licked clean.

The stranger pinned her with serious, dark eyes. "Is there a garage around here?"

Caught by…something in his gaze, Hannah took a moment to process the question. She didn't drive, so she wasn't as familiar with those details as she otherwise would be. "We have two that I know of." Which one would be more likely hiring? "Lou Perkins is over on Grantham Street, about three blocks that way." She pointed toward the north end of the town green. "His nephew just got his second DUI and was shipped off to rehab a couple weeks ago, so he's a little short-handed. And then there's Benny Wills's place on the west side of town." She offered up some quick directions there as well. "There's a gorgeous restored Chevelle sitting out front. You can't miss it."

He watched her for another long moment with that inscrutable gaze before finally muttering, "Thanks."

She gestured to the empty bowl. "Can I get that out of your way?"

The stranger nodded, so she scooped up the dishes with her free hand.

"Sure I can't talk you into some pie?"

"Not right now. Thanks."

She flashed another smile. "Endless refills on coffee. You stay as long as you like."

THOUGH he really needed to get moving, Sergeant Ryan Malone lingered over his coffee and surreptitiously watched the waitress as she continued to decorate the diner's Christmas tree, both because he was wondering how the hell it would turn out, all loaded with forks and spoons, and because he kept expecting to catch a glimpse of elf ears through that fall of dark hair. She'd make a good elf with that fine-boned face and fair skin. She hummed while she worked, the edge of a smile just waiting to bow up those full lips. How could anybody over the age of ten be that unrelentingly cheerful and innocent? She made him feel ancient at twenty-seven, though she was probably close to his age.

He strained to hear the tune and finally recognized "It's Beginning To Look A Lot Like Christmas." Certainly the rest of what he'd seen of Wishful fit the bill. As he'd come into the downtown area, he'd noted the holiday decorations mounted on all the light poles and the twinkle lights wrapped around the denuded trees lining Main Street. People bustled along the sidewalk, toting shopping bags and pretty, wrapped packages. It was about as far as he could get from the war zone he'd been walking in mere days ago, and the switch had him feeling more off balance than the jet lag.

Across the room, Elf Girl plugged in the lights and the tree lit up.

Well, I'll be damned.

The glow of the white twinkle lights bounced off the silverware and gave the tree a warm, inviting glow. He'd never imagined utensils would make good ornaments for a Christmas tree.

Elf Girl stepped back, crossing her arms and beaming in satisfaction. That smile did something to a man. Certainly it had done something to him. He'd had no intention of stopping in the diner. None at all. Then she'd flashed those dimples at him, and he'd been pulled inside as if she were a kerosene heater that could thaw his frozen hands and feet.

She'd thought he was homeless. After traveling for three days straight to get from Bumfuck, Afghanistan to here, he sure as hell looked it. God knew when he'd last shaved. They had relaxed grooming standards where he'd landed this deployment. Exhaustion had carved lines around his eyes. He'd been awake way too damned long even before he boarded the MAC flight back to Fort Polk, where he'd picked up the rust bucket of a truck he'd borrowed from a friend still overseas. Smitty had sworn the thing was ugly but sound and would get him the six hours to Wishful. Ryan had believed him —until the ancient Chevy began to sputter and wheeze when he was nearly to his destination.

The truck had crapped out eight miles from town.

Ryan had left in such a hurry, he had little with him other than his duffle. Not even a coat to face the frigid December weather. And since when was it this freaking cold in Mississippi in December? He'd found an ancient and smelly jacket shoved behind the seat. It had all kinds of questionable stains, but it was another layer against the chill, so he'd put it on and started walking to town. No doubt that hadn't helped with the impression of homelessness.

Too many people would've looked through him, pretending he wasn't there, or gotten nervy, like the other waitress that'd been hiding in the kitchen since he walked in. But not the elf. Her instinct had been to bring him in out of the cold, warm him up, and feed him. She'd met his gaze head-on and hadn't even balked at the stench of the jacket. Wasn't that interesting? Nice to know there were people like her out there in the world, even if he himself wasn't in need of her kindness.

Well, he was thawed out now, and he was losing daylight. If he was gonna get by one of the garages to see about getting a tow, he needed to get moving. Waiting until Elf Girl slipped through the door to the kitchen, Ryan pulled out a wad of cash and left a ridiculous tip —more than enough to cover the soup and coffee—then headed out into the cold.

As it had sounded closer, he took a chance on Lou Perkins's place, trudging north along the town green until he located Grantham Street. The garage wasn't hard to find, and the tow truck he desperately needed was parked right out front. The bay doors were closed, but the single door to the office part of the building was unlocked, so he ducked inside. The office was empty. Some kind of hard rock Christmas music blared from the garage. Following the music, he tugged open another door and stepped into the workspace. A pair of legs was visible beneath an older model Ford Escort. The work boots tapped in time with the music as their owner sang along with more enthusiasm than skill.

"Hello?" Ryan called.

The feet stopped twitching and the creeper shot out from beneath the car. A skinny, balding man with a graying goatee peered up at him. "What can I do ya for?"

"Was hoping you could hook me up with a tow and some repairs. My truck broke down about eight miles from here."

The older man's dark eyes skimmed him from head to toe as he sat up. "You walk all the way here?"

"Yes, sir."

"Reckon you could use some coffee. Pot's on in the office. I gotta finish up here in the next little bit, 'fore Betsy Maynard swings by to pick this puppy up." He tapped the bumper of the Escort. "Then we'll see what there is to see."

Ryan considered calling his uncle Percy. But that'd blow the element of surprise, and given the family's reports of his behavior lately, Ryan wasn't quite ready to give up that advantage.

Resigned to waiting, he just nodded. It'd take less time to do this than to hunt up the other garage. And he was really damned tired. Retreating back to the office, he set down his bag and took one of the thinly padded chairs.

"Hey fella."

Ryan tripped from sleep to wakefulness in an instant, his hand reaching for the combat knife he wasn't actually wearing at the moment.

The mechanic stood a good three paces away, hands lifted in the universal sign for no threat. "Army?"

"Yes, sir." Ryan forced his muscles to relax. He should've heard the mechanic's approach. Damn, he must be more exhausted than he realized.

"Navy," the man said. "Thirty years ago, now. You have the look aboutcha. Ready to go pick up that truck?"

The two of them loaded into the tow truck and Ryan directed the mechanic—who was, in fact, Lou himself—to where he'd left the Chevy on the little two-lane highway. Quick and efficient, Lou had the truck hooked up and towed back to the garage in less than an hour. Then he went the extra mile and dropped Ryan off at Percy's on his way home. Apparently Elf Girl wasn't the only person in town willing to go out of their way to help a stranger.

Shouldering his bag, Ryan strode up the walk toward the house. The porch was dark, but a light shone from somewhere in the back. He pressed the bell, listening to the tones of it ring and fade before a faint voice hollered, "I'm coming. I'm coming!"

He waited, wondering exactly what to say since he hadn't called ahead. Before he could decide, a loud crash sounded from inside.

"Percy?" Ryan shouted. He banged on the door, tested the knob. Locked. He checked the immediate vicinity for a key. Finding none, and given the reports his mom had passed along about the state of Percy's health, he dropped his bag, took a step back, and kicked in the front door.

The lock gave way with a snap, the door

flying back to hit the interior wall. He charged through with all the speed and efficiency of his Delta Force training, clearing rooms until he found the old man on his knees, one hand braced on the arm of a sofa as he struggled to rise. A lamp lay on the floor, the cattywampus shade casting crazy shadows on the wall.

A quick flash of fear crossed Percy's face before he firmed his expression. "Who the hell are you and what are you doing in my house?"

Ryan picked up the lamp and righted it before offering a hand. "Good to see you too, Uncle Percy."

CHAPTER 2

"*I*'m home!" Hannah sang out.

"Back here."

She dumped her purse and went in search of her older sister.

Carolanne stood in the kitchen, the counters covered by the ingredients and equipment of her trade. The apron she wore read *Your OPINION was not in the RECIPE.* She tapped at the screen of the tablet mounted to one of the cabinets, making a notation about whatever recipe she was developing.

"What are you making?"

"Experimenting with some new cookies. I'm wanting something new to pair with the hot cocoa I'm serving this month."

Hannah reached for one of the many aprons her sister had on hand. This one read *I bake because punching people is frowned upon.* "I volunteer as tribute. Does this mean we're having cookies for dinner?"

Carolanne arched a brow. "Was it that kind of day?"

"No, it was actually a really good day. Mama Pearl loved the tree I decorated for the diner. And there was this guy."

The other brow went up. "A guy?"

Hannah waved that off and grabbed a clean spoon from the drawer to scoop up a taste of the dough. "Not that kind of guy. He was homeless." Though that tip hadn't fit with his appearance. "Or maybe not homeless, but down on his luck, I think." But if that was the case, why had he left such a big tip? Pride? Christmas spirit? Maybe she had the whole thing wrong.

She stuck the spoon in her mouth, letting

the sweet and spicy dough melt on her tongue. "Mmm, delicious. What is that?"

"Cardamom and cinnamon. And they'll be studded with roasted pecans, I think."

"I approve." As she rolled dough to Carolanne's specifications, Hannah told her about the soldier.

"You always did have a soft spot for vets."

"Hard not to."

There'd been several homeless veterans in the vicinity of her old design firm's offices in Atlanta. Where other people crossed the street to avoid them or averted their eyes, Hannah had made a habit of bringing something for them. Not a lot. She'd been a junior member of the firm living in an expensive city. But coffee or sandwiches when she could. So when she'd had her accident near there more than a year ago, it'd been those vets who'd rescued her, they who'd first been on the scene.

"I still worry about my guys," she admitted. Without her there, who was watching out for them?

"I'm sure they're finding their way. You did something good for this one, and that's good karma out in the Universe."

"I could use some good karma. I think I'm finally ready to dip a toe back into my actual profession again."

Carolanne's hands paused on the cookie cutter. "Oh?" Her tone was deceptively casual, but that careful, watchful manner was proof she was slipping into therapist mode.

You can take the therapist away from her couch... She didn't suppose her sister would ever lose that training.

"I've been itching to do...something for a while now." In truth, she'd been itchy in general, which wasn't like her. "I'm so grateful to Mama Pearl for hiring me on, but I miss doing my thing. The creativity and challenge of it. So, I figured I'd use the holidays to test the waters."

"How exactly?"

"I'll offer up decorating services to people to help them get their businesses or homes all ready for the holidays. I've already got a notebook with ideas for various businesses down-town. It's on tomorrow's to do list to swing by and talk to the owners and give them my pitch. It'd be pro-bono work, just to spread some holiday cheer and show my skills to the town. And, if I'm lucky, it'll help get me some referrals for some legitimate decorating jobs down the line." She had bigger aspirations than that, but she hadn't quite worked up the courage to go after them. Admitting that to Carolanne would inevitably steer the conversation toward the other fears she was avoiding, so Hannah popped a pecan into her mouth instead.

"Hands off the pecans until we're done," her sister ordered.

With an impish grin, Hannah grabbed one more on principle and made a show of chomping it.

"So you've decided to stay in Wishful instead of going back to Atlanta?"

That was something Hannah had given a great deal of thought over the past months. She'd loved the creative challenges of her job in

Atlanta and loved the city she'd grown up in. But if she went back, she'd be starting over at the bottom of the heap, having to claw her way up all over again, along with all the other junior designers, not all of whom had her sense of fair play. Wishful had taken her in as much as her sister had after the accident. The people here had given her a place and purpose.

"Yeah, I think I have." Maybe she wouldn't have the kind of career opportunities here that she'd have in a big city, but she had other things that were just as valuable to her.

Carolanne fixed steady green eyes on her. "Is it because you really want to stay or because you're afraid to leave?"

That was a question Hannah didn't really want to answer. So she sidestepped it. "Trying to get rid of me, big sis?"

"You know I love having you here, and you can stay as long as you like. I'm just curious, is all."

Just curious, my ass.

"It's past the year mark," Carolanne continued. "You've got a clean bill of health and nothing stopping you from picking up your old life."

"You mean other than lack of a job."

"There are other jobs with other firms."

She'd considered that. "And few of them would be excited about a prospective employee who's spent more than a year out of the field."

"You've got your blog and that whole Pinterest following."

"That's not the same thing." Even if those online outlets had kept her from going insane. "Anyway, that's not the point. I love Wishful, and I'm really happy here."

That wasn't a lie. She *was* happy here. More to the point, she was comfortable here. She loved the people, loved the town. And if it was small enough that it enabled her to continue not driving, well, what was wrong with that?

Carolanne's face set in familiar, neutral lines as she weighed what to say and how to get Hannah to face the things she was avoiding. Before her sister found those words, Hannah offered a bright smile. "Now, let's talk about the fabulous displays you're going to let me create at Sweet Magnolias."

A faint crease formed between Carolanne's brows, but she didn't press. Thank God. "What displays might those be?"

"I was thinking on that wall by the register, I'd make a special display for all your mugs, arrange them so they look like a Christmas tree."

"A Christmas tree?"

Hannah didn't let the skepticism faze her. "Some little shelves of graduated lengths mounted to the wall. Some greenery. The mugs themselves will stand in for ornaments. Trust me. You're gonna love it."

"I can't think of a problem with any of that."

Get them to agree to something small, then go in for the kill. She clapped her hands together and grinned. "Excellent. Now, let's talk gingerbread."

"—BREAKING down doors like some kinda hooligan," Percy groused.

Ryan examined the door frame. Not as bad as it could've been, all things considered. "I thought you were in trouble."

"Trouble? What the hell kind of trouble would I be in in my own house?"

Ryan didn't point out that he'd fallen and could've broken a hip. That wasn't a productive way to start that whole conversation. "My mistake. I'll fix it. Do you have wood glue and some clamps?"

"In the garage."

The garage was one step away from being an episode of *Hoarders*. It took Ryan nearly twenty minutes of searching around the stacks of boxes and jumble of tools before he found what he wanted. That in and of itself was a small miracle. Clearly, Percy needed help with some kind of clean out. If he fell out here, he might get buried under the detritus of...what the hell was all this stuff? Ryan peeked inside one of the boxes and found stacks of *National*

Geographic.

Fire hazard.

Adding it to his mental list, Ryan went back inside to start repairs on the door.

"What the hell are you doing here boy?"

Checking up on you, old man. Not that he could say that. Mom had warned him that Percy had gotten paranoid, cranky, and distrustful of everybody. With none of his own blood kin left—at least none who lived within five hundred miles or gave a damn—it had fallen to his adopted family to keep up with him and his failing health. The way she'd made it sound on the phone, Percy was at death's door, so Ryan had moved heaven and earth to get here to check on him. He and the old man had always been tight, though their communication had been limited during this last tour in Afghanistan. Best he could tell, things weren't near as dire as Mom had made it out to be, but Percy had aged ten years since his wife's funeral two years ago. He was too thin, with deep shadows beneath his eyes, and he probably wasn't eating properly, given his shaky state.

"I'm on leave." And God help him if his CO found out Percy wasn't technically family.

"Well, no shit, you're here instead of there. Why?" He crossed his bony arms. "You got sent, didn't you?"

There wasn't a damned thing wrong with Percy's brain. As confirming that fact would set his mission back even more than it already was, Ryan kept his focus on carefully running glue in the cracks of the door frame to buy himself some time. What excuse would Percy accept that wouldn't have him trying to boot Ryan out as soon as this door was repaired?

"Well?"

"I couldn't go home."

"What's that mean?"

Ryan tightened the clamps. "You know my mother. She'll do the whole welcome the hero home, with a party and every blessed member of the extended family, and probably most of the neighborhood. I couldn't face it." And it was the truth. The very idea of coming up against all that with what he'd been dealing with overseas made his head ache. Hell, last week he'd been clearing out a terrorist cell. He wasn't up to playing that kind of mental whiplash, and he figured Percy—an Army veteran himself— would understand.

The old man grunted. "Your mama know you're stateside?"

"Yes, sir." He carefully scraped away the excess glue.

"Isn't she expecting you?"

"Not yet. I told her I was gonna visit some friends."

"And you're here."

Ryan arched a brow. "You're a friend, last I checked."

"Hmph. Reckon so. How 'bout you go shower and scrape a few layers of that bush off your face? Looks like you haven't had a chance to do it for a while."

"True enough." He pushed the door as far closed as he could get it with the clamps and nudged a chair in front to hold it in place. "This ought to be dry enough to shut in an hour or so. Let me drape a blanket or something to keep the cold air out as well as we can. I think I saw one in the garage."

Ryan rigged up the covering without commentary from the peanut gallery, then scooped up his bag and headed upstairs.

"Guest room is first door on the right."

"Thanks."

The room was dusty, as if nobody had been in there for a while. They probably hadn't. Percy wasn't exactly a social butterfly, having company on any kind of regular basis. If ever. Had anybody been in here since Janie passed two years ago? Maybe a housekeeper to dust once in a blue moon, but certainly the remaining family—all his late wife's side—had all gone back to their lives, as if the moment she'd died, Percy had been excommunicated and no longer deserved their consideration.

Assholes.

Ryan dug out his Dopp kit and laid out his

toiletries on the bathroom counter in a neat grid before turning on the water. As he stepped beneath the spray, he took a long moment to bask in intense gratitude for the solid water pressure and hot spray. Instead of rushing through with the mission-ready efficiency he practiced overseas, he pressed his hands against the tile wall and stood, letting water beat down on him, imagining the layers of grit and grime sluicing off and circling the drain. He wished the invisible film of inhumanity was so easily banished. He believed in the job, believed in the mission, but sometimes—like today when faced with the sweet, basic decency and cheer of Elf Girl—the acute divide between his reality and civilian life reared up to punch him in the gut.

By the time he'd finished the shower and gone after the mountain man beard with scissors and a trimmer until he at least appeared civilized, he wanted nothing more than to fall flat on his face on the full-sized bed. But that wasn't the mission. He couldn't just barge in on Percy and turn into an antisocial hermit. Not to mention, there was still the door to finish with. He'd dress and head downstairs to prepare them both a meal. It was the least he could do to make sure they both got fed properly. Maybe he could start a load of laundry to get rid of the last suggestions of homelessness. And he'd see what was what with his uncle.

Percy was back in his chair, watching some cop show when Ryan got downstairs.

"I'm making supper."

If Percy heard, he didn't acknowledge. Shrugging, Ryan headed into the kitchen. The mess of dishes on the counter pricked at his military neatness. After he'd loaded what seemed like every glass and mug Percy owned into the dishwasher and started it, Ryan dug through the fridge and pantry. Pickings were slim. Coffee. Powdered creamer. A half dozen eggs. Stale bread. Salsa. A moldy hunk of cheese. A few cans of stuff that had expired in the previous president's administration. He tossed those and shook his head.

Damn, if this was all Percy had in the house,

no wonder he was so thin. What had the guy been eating? Was it a money thing? Did he not know how to fend for himself without his wife to do all the domestic stuff?

Ryan added *Trip to market* to his running mental list. There ought to be enough cheese to salvage for an omelet.

Percy wandered in as he was dumping the beaten eggs into a skillet. "What's that?"

"Gonna be dinner. You should start a grocery list. I'll make a run tomorrow." He nodded toward a notepad on the counter.

"Could've ordered pizza."

"Is that what you've been eating on?" He added a few more items to the list himself.

Percy shuffled over to pour himself a glass of water, then sank into one of the ladder-back chairs at the kitchen table. "Sometimes. Don't much like cooking."

"Well, this won't be like Aunt Janie's cooking, but I don't think we'll starve. Kinda late, but you want coffee?"

"No. How long are you stayin', son?"

Ryan paused. "You trying to kick me out?"

"Just asking a question."

"I don't know. I borrowed a truck from a buddy. It broke down a few miles outside town. The mechanic is supposed to get to it tomorrow, and he'll let me know how long it'll be. But I figured so long as I was crashing your hospitality, I could help out around the house."

Bushy, gray brows drew together. "Help out?"

"I'm no good at sitting still. The Army's made sure of that. I figure you've got some stuff that needs doing—a second set of hands or a younger back or whatever. Thought I'd earn my keep." Ryan cut the omelet in half and slid each onto a plate.

Percy eyed the food before lifting his gaze back to Ryan's. "Reckon we can come up with something."

Well, that was a start. Ryan would take it.

CHAPTER 3

"You know, I'm not normally a fan of any sort of project that destroys books, but I have to admit, this looks kind of amazing."

From her position in the front window of Inglenook Books, Hannah smiled over at Reed Campbell, the owner, as she finished adding the last layer of "branches" to the Christmas tree she'd fashioned out of book pages. "Well, it's certainly not something you'd do with new stock, but giving new life to a book that's already damaged…yeah, there's a lot you can do with pages. The print against the white makes for a cool effect. I'll be making a wreath, too."

Brenda, the bookstore's only other employee, wandered over. "Where did you learn how to do all this? Pinterest?"

"There are certainly plenty of ideas there," Hannah conceded, "but no, I'm actually an interior decorator by training. I've got a degree from the Savannah College of Art and Design."

Her brows drew together in confusion. "And you're working at the *diner?*"

Hannah draped white twinkle lights with way more care than was really necessary until she could get her reaction under control. "I had some health problems that necessitated I leave my job in Atlanta last year. My sister was kind enough to let me stay with her while I got back on my feet, and Mama Pearl has been awesome enough to give me a job. So yeah, I work at the diner, for now."

"Well, I'm just gonna say your talents are wasted," Reed declared. "I wish you'd let me pay you in more than filched snacks from the knitting club."

Hannah flashed him a smile. "That's not what this was about. I wanted the opportunity to use my skills for fun to spread some Christmas cheer and advertise my capabilities. You're taking a chance on me by letting me do this." And, okay, maybe part of this whole thing was about reminding herself that she still *had* the skills. The last year had been a massive earthquake to her confidence. But already she had two more appointments to discuss holiday window displays—one with Brides and Belles and another with Edison Hardware.

"I'm definitely getting the better end of the deal. And at the very least you permanently have the friends and family discount for whatever you buy."

"Deal. Which works out well because I'll be back for some Christmas shopping."

"Are you thinking about opening your own design firm?" Reed asked.

"Maybe someday," she hedged. But wasn't that exactly what she ultimately hoped to do? "I'm a long way from having the capital for something like that." The accident had seen to that.

"You should go talk to my cousin Mitch's wife, Tess, over at the small business incubator, when she gets back from maternity leave. I know they've still got some space."

Given she worked in the primary gossip hub in town, Hannah remembered hearing something about that. "What exactly *is* a small business incubator?"

"Tess can explain it better than I can, but basically it gives infrastructure and mentorship to small businesses to help them get off the ground. It gives you a safety net you wouldn't have going out entirely on your own."

That sounded...intriguing. The idea of having a mentor guide her through the business side of things made her feel a lot less frightened of the prospect. "But they aren't letting just anybody in, right? It wouldn't be just signing a lease on space."

"No, there's an application process. They've got more info on the website. I'll jot it down for you."

"Thanks, I appreciate it."

The bell over the door jangled and a herd of chattering, blue-haired ladies wandered in. The Casserole Patrol was a familiar fixture at Dinner Belles. In her tenure there, they'd opined on the love lives of literally everybody in town. Young, old. Didn't matter. It was their favorite occupation. They consistently hoped that camping out in the back booth nearest the kitchen would somehow give them a leg up in winning the assorted betting pools Omar was constantly running on who would end up with whom. Plenty of people found the trio annoying. For Hannah it was like having her own, local version of the Golden Girls. That certainly didn't stop Reed's sales clerk, Brenda, from beating a hasty retreat to the stock room in back before they noticed her.

"Reed Campbell, you are still on my poop list!" Miss Delia crowed.

Hannah went brows up at this assertion.

Reed didn't bat an eye. "Now, Miss Delia, I can't help Cecily wanted to have the wedding in Greenwich."

Miss Betty's face fell. "I guess we can't expect her to want to have the wedding here with her family all up north." This was pronounced in a tone that suggested that "up north" was as bad as being from a third world country.

If there was one thing the Casserole Patrol loved more than gossiping about love lives, it was watching those lives being joined in holy matrimony…and dissecting the weddings and receptions later for who might've hooked up with whom and who had a bun in the oven.

Reed, ever the diplomat, put an arm around Miss Betty's shoulders. "I'll see if I can set up a time for you to see the wedding pictures."

Miss Maudie Bell, the third member of their trio, nodded in approval. "You do that."

"Is there anything I can get y'all before the rest of the knitting club arrives? The coffee's already ready in the kitchen."

"If you could dig up a plate for these cookies we got from the bakery, that would be great, sugar." Miss Delia patted him on the cheek and offered the box from Sweet Magnolias.

"Oh, are those the new sugar and spice cookies?" Hannah asked.

"They are," Miss Delia confirmed.

"I can vouch that they are awesome. Carolanne used me as taste tester the other night."

"Your sister certainly is a whiz in the kitchen," Miss Betty declared, shuffling over to the window. "What is all this?"

"I'm simultaneously spreading some Christmas cheer and the word that I am actually an interior decorator. I'm offering up my services for shops and homes for the cost of supplies." Hopefully the small hand-lettered notes with her name and contact number at the bottom of the assorted window displays would net some more requests.

"What a good idea. For home stuff, are you working with what people already have?"

"I certainly can. Part of the fun of decorating is making something new and interesting out of what's already on hand."

"I need to look into that," Miss Maudie Bell muttered.

"What, you can't get Chester to help put up the tree?" Miss Betty asked.

There'd been a bit of friction in the ranks since Maudie Bell had invited Chester Harkin to move in a few months before. Throwing a man into the mix had messed with the Three Musketeers vibe the ladies had going on.

"Well sure, he'd put it up, but he's a man, after all. Pretty is not his forte. And as the family is coming to us this year, I'd like to make a fine showing."

Hannah smiled. "I'd be happy to help you with that, if you'd like."

"I just might do that."

"When's Chester gonna make an honest woman out of you?" Miss Delia asked.

"Land sakes, it took me years to housetrain my first husband. Why would I want to go complicating things by marrying Chester?"

Miss Maudie Bell unwrapped her scarf and began wandering back toward the cluster of sofas where the knitting club was due to have their meeting. "Besides, he hasn't asked, and it's kind of fun scandalizing the kids."

Hannah held in a snicker as Miss Delia wandered off. She realized the third Musketeer had lingered. "Miss Betty, was there something I could help you with?"

"Could I hire out your services as a gift to someone else? I've got a friend who could really use a dose of Christmas cheer."

"I'd be delighted to help. What did you have in mind?"

"TAKE OFF YOUR SHIRT."

"I'm not some five-dollar date you picked up off base."

Ryan pinned Percy with a flat stare. "First off, I have never had to pay for my dates. Second, you said yourself you haven't had a physical since Aunt Janie passed. Unless you want me to toss your bony ass over my shoulder and carry you in to the doctor fireman-style, you'll take off your shirt and let me examine you."

Percy crossed his arms and glared. "I'm perfectly healthy."

"Then you've got nothing to hide. An exam will get Mom off your back *and* mine." He'd spent the last two days trying to do a proper check-up on the old man and Percy had stymied him at every turn.

"You scared of your little ol' mama?"

"Damned straight. She's a helluva lot scarier than my CO." Ryan could take yelling. He could take verbal abuse and dressing down. What he couldn't take was his mother's profound disappointment if anything happened to Percy on his watch.

His uncle made a rude noise. "And you call yourself Delta Force."

Irritated, Ryan straightened. "Aunt Janie didn't put up with this shit from you."

"Janie looked a helluva lot better in lingerie

than you. And anyway, she's not here anymore to make me." His chin lifted in defiance, but Ryan caught the faint tremble in his tone and felt like an asshole.

Her death had cut Percy off at the knees, and the man hadn't recovered. There was no statute of limitations on grief. Ryan understood that well enough, even if the ones he'd lost had been friends instead of lovers. There'd been so many, and the burden of that stuck with him. He couldn't imagine the pain of losing his other half. Not that he had another half. But fine. He'd stop pushing. For now.

He zipped his medical bag closed again and tried to figure out how to steer the conversation away from this emotional quicksand.

Percy, apparently, had other ideas. "You'd do better to spend your leave finding your own self a woman."

Unbidden, an image of Elf Girl popped into Ryan's head, with those big blue eyes and that smile that wouldn't quit. She was his absolute antithesis—all sweetness and light. And he had no business even thinking about the likes of her.

"I don't need a woman."

"Son, we all need a woman. 'Specially in the military. It gets damned cold in the desert. And the heart gets frozen besides. Has to, to do what you do."

That was the damned truth. There was no other way to survive the kinds of missions Special Forces ran. War wasn't for the weak or emotional.

"There's no room for attachments in war."

"On the battlefield, no. But every man needs to be reminded of his humanity. A woman'll do that."

Several members of Ryan's team had wives and girlfriends. They kept pictures of them, tucked into their helmets or inside flak jackets. Most of those photos were frayed around the edges from all the handling. Some even had the faces all but worn away from stroking, seeking that grounding, that comfort, in the dark, desperate times. Their women were beacons of hope. The thing they were fighting to get home to.

He'd never had that. Never wanted it. Oh, he had plans for finding a woman someday. After he got out of the Army, once he'd used his GI Bill to go on to medical school. But that was for the future, when he wasn't spending his days up to his armpits in battle trauma. When he had bandwidth to think about something other than the mission or the brothers in arms he hadn't been able to save. As medic, he faced down more death than most, and it was hard not to take a piece of every case with him.

"Where'd your brain get to, son?"

Ryan shook himself. "Nothin'. Just trying to remember how long it's been since I had an actual date." A lie, but now that he'd said it, he did wonder. He'd had the occasional bedmate for the night on leave, but the last time he'd had more than a physical release had been…damn. Three years?

"If you gotta think that hard about it, it's been too damned long."

As that hit too close to the truth, Ryan turned the tables. "What about you, old man? Have you thought about getting out there and dating again?"

Percy looked at him as if he'd just suggested running stark naked down Main Street.

Ryan couldn't imagine how hard this had to be on him, but Percy needed to be nudged back into living. "It's been two years."

The gnarled hand fisted. "I know how long it's been since the fucking cancer took my Janie."

"She wouldn't expect you to stay alone."

"That woman was the love of my life. I won't insult her memory by looking for another."

Open mouth, insert foot. Ryan ran a hand over the hair he'd managed to get cut yesterday and wished he could take that back.

"What'd Lou say about that truck?"

Oh, yeah, he'd definitely lost ground in this battle of wills. He was grateful he didn't have to lie. "The part's on backorder. It's supposed to be in early next week, so unless you expect me to hitchhike to my mama's, you're stuck with me for at least a few more days."

Percy grunted. "Reckon I can put you to work."

"Reckon you can."

"I still say you ought to get your ass out there and find a woman."

"And where exactly do you think I'm gonna pick up a nice girl for just a week or two?" No reason to mention he was blowing through the lion's share of his accumulated leave to be here.

"I don't rightly know, but I expect if you pull your head out of your ass, you stand a much better chance of finding one."

The ring of the doorbell interrupted whatever sarcastic retort Ryan might have made. Just as well. They needed to get the hell off the topic of his love life. "I'll get it."

Crossing over to the freshly repainted door, he tugged it open to find his cutie pie waitress from the diner standing on the front porch.

Santa, you've got a helluva sense of humor.

CHAPTER 4

The cheerful, professional spiel poised on Hannah's tongue evaporated as she came face to face with the soldier from Dinner Belles, who clearly was *not* homeless. He'd cleaned up, having showered, shaved, and gotten a haircut. And dear God, without that mountain man beard and several layers of smell, he was hot. A gray henley stretched across well-defined muscles and the close-cropped reddish-brown beard highlighted a strong jaw. Her fingers itched to trace it.

Say something.

"Hi!"

One brow arched faintly.

Okay so maybe she sounded a little like Will Farrell from *Elf*. But what was she supposed to say to the man? She'd treated him like he was homeless. How was she supposed to apologize for that assumption? *Should* she apologize? Or was this one of those gaffes she should just let go and pray nobody ever brought it up again? This was not a topic that Emily Post or Martha Stewart ever covered.

"Can I help you?" His voice was a low rumble. Added to the unexpected hotness, the timbre of it seemed to reach out and stroke along her spine.

Get a freaking grip!

Needing one in a very literal sense, she clutched the ends of her scarf as if it were somehow an anchor in this extremely awkward social situation. "I'm Hannah Wheeler. I'm sorry to bother you, but I've been sent by a secret Santa to decorate your house for the holidays." She was too bubbly, but she couldn't seem to stop herself from babbling. "It's this thing I've been doing around town—mostly window displays for local businesses, but someone asked me to stop by here to spread some Christmas cheer and—" Catching the glint of amusement in those serious chestnut eyes, she managed to cut herself off. "You're not Percy, are you?"

"I am not." Again with the rumbly tones.

Hannah's knees wobbled. *For heaven's sake, girl, you act like you've never heard a deep voice before. Pull yourself together.* Hoping she wasn't drooling, she checked out what she could see of the dim interior. "Do I have the wrong house?"

"Nope." He stepped back, opening the door wider and gesturing her inside.

She hesitated in the entryway, noting the scent of fresh paint and wondering what had been updated about the house. The whole place felt neglected and a little worn around the edges. Sad. Which fit with what Miss Betty had told her about its occupant. No wonder she'd been moved to intervene.

Soldier Hottie led her down the hall. She tried not to stare at his butt, she really did. But his cargo pants displayed it so well. The sight of it forcibly reminded her that driving wasn't the only thing she hadn't done in more than a year.

You are not breaking that streak right now and not with this guy. Eyes up, cupcake.

She managed to jerk them skyward a second before her guide turned to gesture her into a living room. Spying the old man encamped in an ancient recliner, she forced her feet into motion and fixed a smile firmly in place. "Percy Gannaway?"

"Yes?" He eyed her with all the wariness he might show a feral cat that wandered into his house.

"I'm Hannah Wheeler. I'm an interior designer, and I've been sent as a gift to decorate your house for the holidays."

"Interior designer?" This from Soldier Hottie. "I thought you were a waitress."

She glanced at him. "I am also a waitress at the moment."

"That explains the utensil tree."

"It does, yes." She couldn't tell from his inflection whether he actually liked the little tree at Dinner Belles or not.

A frown carved deep lines around Percy's pinched mouth. "Who sent you?"

Shifting her attention back to him, she dialed up the smile, remembering Miss Betty's insistence on remaining anonymous. "I can't tell. It's a Christmas surprise."

Confusion and no little amount of suspicion darkened the old man's face. "You're not selling anything?"

"No, sir. Just trying to spread some Christmas cheer. I came by this afternoon to find out when would be a convenient time to decorate."

He wanted to say no. The intention was written clearly on his face. So she pulled out the thing Miss Betty had assured her would change his mind. "I understand your house used to be one of the big showpieces in town come Christmas."

His expression softened a fraction. "My late wife loved Christmas. People used to come from all over to drive by our place."

"It was a helluva sight," Soldier Hottie agreed.

What exactly was his connection to Percy? Miss Betty had said he had no family, so who was this guy? Didn't matter. She wasn't here about him. As gently as she could, Hannah smiled. "She sounds like she was a lovely woman. Wouldn't this be a nice way to bring back a piece of her for the holidays? A tribute to the season she loved so much?"

Percy's gaze turned speculative. "I haven't much bothered with Christmas since she passed."

Oh, that made her heart hurt. She loved Christmas so very much. She couldn't fathom not celebrating at all. "I know it can be difficult. My first few Christmases after my Nana passed were really hard. I get my love of the holidays from her and it simply wasn't the same without her there, in the middle of everything. But my sister and I always make her special iced butter cookies, and it brings her a little closer to us."

He went silent, his face shuttering, and she wondered if she'd gone too far. Maybe the loss was still too raw for discussion of traditions. Or maybe the fact that he had no one left to share those traditions with made his situation totally different.

When Percy straightened, his jaw set in a stubborn line, she expected a *Thanks, but no thanks.* Instead, he nodded. "You know what? You're right. She'd be disappointed I haven't kept things up without her. Let's do it up big. Pull out all the stops."

Hannah beamed. "I'd be absolutely delighted to do that."

"You're gonna need some help. I'm not as agile as I used to be—damned bursitis. But Ryan here is more than capable. He can be your assistant."

"I can do what now?" Soldier Hottie—Ryan —lost that flat expression and unfolded his arms.

"Help haul things out of the attic, string the lights, carry in the tree. It's gotta be a live one. My Janie wouldn't stand for anything else." There was some kind of challenge in the gaze Percy fixed on him. "You did say you wanted to help out."

Why did she think there was something more to this whole thing than the simple words implied? "I don't want to be a bother."

"No bother at all, young lady. We could both use a little Christmas spirit in our lives."

For just a moment, Ryan's jaw tensed, as if he wanted to argue. Instead, he flashed a wry smile at Percy. "I guess you'll have to hand over the keys so I can go pick up the tree."

"Sorry, I think you mean 'we,'" Hannah interrupted. "You're not picking out a tree without me." Because, damn, if she was going to get the chance to really pull out all the stops, she was gonna make this house a Christmas showstopper.

"My mistake." The wry smile turned genuine as he shifted his attention to her.

The punch of it nearly knocked her off her feet.

Oh, I am in deep, deep trouble.

Percy let out a rusty chuckle. "Oh, my Janie would've liked you. I'll go get the keys."

IF ANYBODY HAD ASKED Ryan last week what he'd be doing today, the very last thing he'd have imagined was wandering a Christmas tree lot with a woman who'd clearly escaped from the set of one of those Hallmark Channel Christmas movies his mother loved so much. Between her unwavering good cheer and the candy-cane-striped scarf and hat, Hannah was a walking, talking holiday card. It should've been annoying. Nobody could be that happy and have even a toe still dipped in the real world.

But she'd made Percy smile. Hell, she'd made *him* smile, even if it was at his own expense because Percy was playing matchmaker. Just what would his Elf Girl say if she knew about that? And why the hell was he thinking of her as his? They were nothing to each other but two people helping out his uncle.

As they reached the end of the row, she lifted her hand in a wave to the guy handling the money. "Hey Jace."

The guy grinned. "Back again?"

"Yep!"

"How many trees have you decorated?" Ryan asked.

"This is my fourth one this week, in addition to three storefronts on Main Street."

"We ought to be giving you the frequent shopper discount," Jace told her.

"I'm coming after one of the big ones this time. I need at least a ten-footer."

"Those will be down this way. C'mon." Jace leapt up.

Ryan wondered whether his Mr. Helpful streak was due to her having been here several times already or because they had a thing. They were on a first-name basis after all. And why should that bug him? He had no claim on this woman.

"Where's Tara tonight?" Hannah asked.

"It's the last week of rehearsals before *The Nutcracker*, so she's at the studio. Ginny is crazy excited."

"I bet she is! She's been talking about it since this summer to everybody that'll listen." Hannah glanced toward Ryan. Well, more like his shoulder. "Tara is Jace's fiancée. Ginny is her little sister."

Was he supposed to say something about that? He didn't know these people.

Hannah turned her attention back to Jace. "When are you making Ginny your sister in law?"

"It'll be official in May."

So no thing with Hannah. Not that it mattered one way or the other. It was just idle curiosity. Info gathering, in case Ryan decided to get his flirt on. Just to remind himself that he still knew how.

"You'll find all the ten feet and up trees

along this row." Jace glanced at the family of five that spilled out of a minivan. "Do you need help checking things out?"

Ryan stepped up. "I've got it."

"You just let me know when you find the one you want." He wandered off to help the newcomers.

"How you wanna do this?" Ryan asked.

Hannah kept her focus on the trees instead of him. They were arranged loosely in open stalls, each one leaning against the framework. "If you could just pull out the ones I point to and hold them up so I can check whether the trunk is straight and assess the fullness, that'd be great." A blush suffused her cheeks as her gaze slid away.

What was that about?

She pointed to one. He slipped his hand through the branches and grasped the trunk, tugging it vertical.

"Crooked."

He put the tree back and grabbed the next one she pointed to. As she studied the fall of the branches or whatever, he asked, "So are you gonna tell me who asked you to do this?"

She made a gesture for him to spin the tree. "Can you keep a secret?"

Given his entire career involved covert operations, he kinda had a lock on that. "Yes."

"The woman who had the idea was one of Percy's wife's best friends. She's a widow herself and she knows Christmas is the hardest time for him, so she wanted to do something that would maybe help with that."

"That's a helluva nice thing to do." Was Wishful just that kind of community or was he so far removed from kindness that any of it surprised him?

"It is," Hannah agreed, pointing to another tree. "But I kind of wonder if there isn't maybe a little crush involved."

"Yeah?" Maybe Ryan would get the chance at a little payback effort in the matchmaking department. Unlike him, Percy could really use it.

"I could be wrong, but there was something in her eyes when she asked me. I don't know.

She wanted to remain anonymous, so I'm not gonna mess with that and you shouldn't either."

He wasn't making any promises there.

"So how exactly are you related to Percy? Miss—the woman who hired me led me to believe he didn't have any family."

"He doesn't have any close family. Leastwise, not blood kin. He's basically my great uncle, in a complicated Southern sort of way."

"Family you adopted?"

He picked up the next tree and nodded. "He and my grandfather were tight from the time they were knee-high. They stayed close, even after each of them married. Percy and Janie— that'd be his late wife—never had kids, so they sort of adopted my mom and her brothers. The two of them were always in and out of our lives."

Hannah shook her head at the tree, and he put it back. "It's nice of you to come visit him. It's awful when people are alone for the holidays."

"My visit isn't entirely altruistic. His health

has been declining and my mom's worried about him. I got sent to check on him because he's rejected everybody else. Not that I can blame him. At the first mention of assisted living, a guy as independent as Percy digs in his heels. He's been in that house for forty-five years."

"So you're—what?—supposed to talk him into it?"

"I'm supposed to assess whether he really needs it or not."

"And if he does?"

"We'll cross that bridge when we get there."

Throughout the exchange, she stayed way more focused on the task of finding the perfect tree than seemed necessary. He pulled out and put back almost every one in the size category and other than that one, brief glance, she didn't seem to be able to meet his gaze. After her directness at the diner, the shift in behavior seemed out of character.

"What is it?" he demanded.

"What?" Her voice had that high, bright quality again.

"We're supposed to be working together on this thing. That means sometime you're going to have to actually look at me."

The pink in her cheeks deepened and she sucked in a breath. "Okay, I deserved that." Straightening her shoulders, she lifted her gaze to his. The earnestness there was almost painful. "I want to apologize for how I treated you at the diner the other day."

He frowned. Was she remembering something different than he was? "Why? For treating me like a human being with dignity and value?"

She winced. "I thought you were homeless."

Okay, yeah, he'd gotten that. And he'd been impressed with how she'd handled the situation. "In your defense, I totally looked it that day."

"Still. I shouldn't have assumed."

"You assumed I was cold and hungry, and you fed me out of your own pocket. That was a kind thing, and my mama always says you should never apologize for a kindness. Even if you jumped to the wrong conclusion."

The corner of her mouth twitched in a self-deprecating smile. "Your mom sounds like a wise woman."

He tried not to fixate on that mouth, but he really wanted to see those dimples again. "She is. She'd also tell me I owe you a thank you for the meal."

"You thanked me at the diner. *And* left an exorbitant tip. So thank *you.*" She gestured to the tree in his hand. "That one's perfect."

"I'd like to take you to dinner." Wait, what were these words falling out of his mouth? He hadn't planned on asking her out. But how else was he going to get the time to coax out those dimples?

Hannah angled her head and there went the smile. Her dimples winked on like stars. One. Two. "How do you feel about pizza?"

"How do you feel about tonight?"

CHAPTER 5

"If there is a more perfect food than pizza, I don't know what it is." Ryan leaned back in his chair, more relaxed than Hannah had ever seen him, though he still had that watchfulness that told her he'd noticed every single patron and employee of Speakeasy Pizzeria and cataloged their position.

"I would like to submit tacos to that category. But it would be a pretty close race." She eyed the last slice of pizza. Would eating it make her look like a glutton?

"It's all yours. I inhaled more than my fair share."

Taking him at his word, she grabbed it up, wondering if this was supposed to be a date.

He'd come to the house to pick her up, but both Percy and Carolanne lived so close to downtown, they'd walked. It was a work night, and while Hannah didn't keep quite the God-awful baker's hours her sister did, she was still on morning shift and had to be up at the butt crack of dawn. She ought to be pajamaficated and getting ready for bed. Instead, she found herself wishing they could draw the evening out just a little longer. Conversation had been surprisingly easy, if not particularly personal. They'd talked movies and books, music and food. When he unbent from that stoicism she'd observed, Ryan Malone was actually pretty charming. She couldn't decide which one was his natural inclination.

"So how exactly does a waitress get into decorating?"

Oh, so now they were going to actually get

to know each other? "It's more like how does an interior decorator get into waitressing."

He inclined his head. "Okay. How does an interior decorator get into waitressing?"

To buy herself some time, she bit into the pizza. This wasn't something she talked about. She'd been in Wishful for more than a year now, and other than Carolanne and Mama Pearl, nobody really knew why she was here. But she wanted to know more about Ryan, and that was probably going to take a little quid pro quo.

"I graduated with my degree in interior design five years ago and ended up taking an internship at one of the best design firms in Atlanta. It was cutthroat and absolutely insane. Imagine *The Devil Wears Prada,* except not fashion."

His lips twitched. "I'll have to take your word on that one."

"Ruthless, long-hours, no-excuses."

"I'm familiar with that sort of environment." Something in his expression told her his version of those things was very, very different.

"Anyway, after a year, I managed to get my foot in the door with the firm, and I spent the next three years, working my way through the ranks, shooting for junior partner." She flashed a wry smile. "Having no life."

Ryan shifted forward, leaning toward her. "Something happened."

She nibbled on more of the pizza, though the memory of what came next killed the last of her appetite. "Fourteen months ago, while I was on my way to work, I had a seizure and lost control of my car. I didn't actually know that's what was happening at the time, and I don't actually remember the accident. It was a miracle I didn't kill anybody, including myself."

"Were you injured?"

"Whiplash, a concussion, a broken arm. I had some complications with the arm that could have been so much worse, but I happened to crash right near my office. There was this group of homeless veterans that hung out near the parking garage I used, and I'd see them most days. We were friendly. I'd bring them stuff from time to time, so they knew me, knew my car. When I crashed, they came running. One of them had been a medic in the army and was able to stabilize me until the ambulance arrived. He saved my life."

Something flickered in his gaze. "So the soup was paying it forward?"

She shrugged. "Maybe a little. I haven't seen my guys since I left Atlanta. When I got out of the hospital, my doctor told me I couldn't drive for a year, until they'd confirmed the seizure was a fluke. As you might imagine, that doesn't work in Atlanta. So I ended up coming here and moving in with my sister while I recovered. The firm wasn't interested in holding my job."

"Well that's shitty."

Hannah's lips curved at his summation of the situation. "Yeah. But it hasn't been all bad. I love Wishful, and it's been great to spend more time with Carolanne—that's my sister."

"You said you couldn't drive for a year and

that it's been fourteen months. Have you had more seizures?"

"No. It seems to have been one and done."

"But you haven't gone back to Atlanta." Leave it to him to zero in on the thing her sister had been dancing around for two months.

"No." Not wanting to talk any more about that, she changed the subject. "So you were a soldier?"

Ryan settled back in his chair, picking up his iced tea. "Am a soldier. Army."

"Oh yeah? What do you do?" When he didn't answer, she grinned. "Is it one of those 'I'd tell you but then I'd have to kill you' kind of jobs?"

His face settled into something that wasn't quite the stoic mask she'd first seen, but was definitely a major step back from the easy flirtation he'd pulled out over dinner. "Something like that."

Was he teasing? She couldn't read him, but she didn't think so. "You're really going to leave it at that?"

"Yep."

Not sure where to go with that, she was grateful when their waitress came with the check.

By the time they stepped outside, the sun had long since gone down and downtown was mostly deserted, as even businesses with extended holiday hours had closed. She really needed to be getting home to bed, but she wanted to take a little detour first. "Let's walk for a bit."

Ryan fell into step beside her as she crossed the street to the town green. He remained silent as they strolled past the town Christmas tree, spearing into the sky across from City Hall, its lights casting a gorgeous golden glow against the night. She wondered if she'd struck a sore spot by asking about his job. He'd shut down at the mention of it. Or maybe it had simply made him think about other, far less pleasant things. She had no idea what he'd seen, what he'd been forced to do in the name of duty or survival. Such things could haunt a person. Those were the kind of ghosts that had contributed to her guys in Atlanta staying on the streets rather than fully reintegrating into civilian life. A part of her itched to take his hand, to offer him some warmth and human connection. But his hands were shoved into the pockets of his coat.

She stopped at the edge of the burbling fountain. "It's beautiful, isn't it?"

"Looks old."

"They built it just after the Civil War and sourced the water from Hope Springs. That's why the town is called Wishful. Local legend says if you make a wish, it will come true."

Amusement lit his eyes. "Has yours?"

"I haven't made one." But plenty of other people had. Coins glimmered beneath the water, like some kind of mermaid's treasure.

He dug into his pocket and pulled out a coin, offering it to her. "No time like the present."

Surprised, she searched his face. "You don't strike me as a guy who'd believe much in wishes."

"I'm not. But you strike me as a woman who does."

She narrowed her eyes. "Because I'm dreamy and impractical? Not grounded?"

"Hopeful. I figure the world needs more people like you in it." Reaching for her hand, Ryan folded the coin into it. Despite the cold, heat raced up her arm from where his fingers still curled around hers. Awareness slid through her, warm and sweet as molasses.

She really wanted this to be a date.

He jerked his head toward the fountain and released her hand. "Go ahead."

Already regretting the loss of his touch, she turned to face the water. What should she wish for? She had everything she wanted for herself already. Her career goals seemed like way too selfish a thing to waste a wish on. And he'd given her the nickel as if he couldn't make a wish for himself. So by rights, it seemed she should wish something for him. She closed her eyes, still feeling the heat of his.

I wish for Ryan to find the true spirit of Christmas and spread it to Percy along the way.

She upended her palm over the basin, hearing the nickel splash. Okay, so maybe that was a little bit selfish as a wish. Because who better to show them the spirit of Christmas than her? She'd get to spend a little more time with him, maybe burrow under a few more of those layers of reserve. And even if nothing else came of it, she'd get the pleasure of making them both smile.

He was still watching her as she shifted toward him.

"I've got an early day tomorrow. Walk me home?"

Ryan nodded and offered his arm. She tucked her hand in the crook of his elbow, feeling far warmer than the contact accounted for. The walk back went way too fast, despite the fact that they spoke little. The quality of the silence was different somehow. A little easier.

As they stepped up onto the porch, she was back to wondering about the exact status of their evening. Hannah hesitated under the porch light for a moment before digging out her keys, but he didn't make a move to close the distance between them. Maybe the date vibe was just a figment of her imagination. Shoving the key into the lock, she twisted, opening the door a scant inch. "Thanks for dinner."

"Thanks for the company. I enjoyed it."

She waited a moment longer, just in case, then shoved the door open further. Better to get inside before she did or said something to embarrass herself. "I'll see you tomorrow. You be sure to get that tree in water."

"Already done."

"Right. Well then. Goodnight." She stepped backward into the house, tripping over the rug as she went. "I'm okay!"

The low rumble of his laugh made her cheeks burn. "Goodnight, Hannah."

She looked back up at him, liking the sound of her name on his lips. "Night, Ryan."

He gifted her with a sudden smile that

stunned her brain like a flash grenade. "See you tomorrow, Elf Girl."

Before she could get her neurons firing again, he was halfway back up the walk. "Elf Girl?"

Ryan turned around, still grinning. "It seemed appropriate, what with all the Christmas cheer. Bonus points if you show up tomorrow with striped tights and a hat."

Shaking her head with a rueful smile, she shut the door. The man had no idea who he was talking to.

I SHOULD'VE KISSED HER.

The moment he'd walked away from Hannah's door last night, he'd wanted to kick himself. The kiss that hadn't been had haunted his dreams and reminded him it had been way too long since he'd really *wanted* to kiss a woman and take his time about it. Which was exactly why he hadn't done it. He didn't live here. He wouldn't be here longer than another couple of weeks. Hannah Wheeler deserved better than the short-term attentions of a guy like him. But knowing he'd done the right thing hadn't stopped him from wondering how she'd taste, how that long, silky hair would feel in his hands. It hadn't stopped him from feeling like she was the best kind of surprise on Christmas morning—the gift you didn't know you wanted until it showed up pretty and perfect with a big red bow. Which just had him picturing her in that big red bow—and nothing else.

"For a guy who's spent all morning cleaning out flower beds and burning yard trash, you're in an awfully good mood." Percy's voice pulled him out of his musings.

Just as well. Fresh from the shower, Ryan peeked out the back door to make sure the smoldering remains of the burn pile were well-contained. "What makes you say that?"

"You've been whistling."

Had he? It didn't sound like him, but he had

been thinking about Hannah and that smile of hers while he worked.

Percy smirked. "Reckon that has something to do with a certain little brunette you had dinner with last night."

Ryan didn't even dignify that with a response, instead moving past his uncle into the kitchen to grab the pitcher of tea from the fridge.

"I told ya you needed a woman."

"I do not *have* a woman. Nor will I be here long enough to acquire one." And if he regretted that a little, well, he was only human, and he'd enjoyed Hannah's company. He poured a glass and shoved the pitcher back into the fridge a little rougher than necessary.

"Mmmhmm." Percy just continued to watch him with eyes that were too shrewd.

This was all his fault. Ryan hadn't been thinking about a woman at all until his uncle had brought it up. Now he'd probably be taking images of one back with him, whether he wanted to or not. Not ideal considering he'd probably never see Hannah again after he left Wishful. But saying anything about that to Percy would open the door to merciless teasing and additional attempts at matchmaking. Ryan needed to do some more investigating himself to see whether his uncle's mysterious benefactor did indeed have a little crush on him. If she did, well, some diversionary tactics were in order.

The doorbell rang, saving Ryan from having to answer. He gestured to Percy with his glass as he headed to the door. "Behave yourself."

"Where's the fun in that?"

Even as he fixed the older man with a quelling stare, a part of Ryan was happy to see the lighter side. If trying to play matchmaker would help pull Percy out of his funk, he'd suffer—or maybe enjoy—the consequences.

Hannah stood on the front porch, an impish smile making those dimples wink. Perched atop her head was a red and green striped hat—with elf ears attached to the sides.

Though rusty with disuse, his own mouth

tugged up into an answering smile. "You found your ears."

"Seemed appropriate."

Abruptly, he took in the rest of her, realizing her arms were laden with so many bags she shouldn't have been able to keep her feet. Reaching forward to relieve her of the burden, he noted there was no car in the driveway. "How did you get all this here?"

She dialed up that ray of sunshine smile. "I walked, silly."

Ryan blinked. The year-long ban on driving had been up for a couple of months. Did this mean she hadn't started again? Telling himself it wasn't his business, he curled his fingers around the entire wad of bag handles in her left hand. "Give it up, Hercules. Why didn't you call? I'd have come to pick you up."

"Well, I didn't have your number, and it's really not that heavy." She released her grip and he was surprised to find she was right. The load wasn't anywhere near what he expected.

"What's in here anyway?"

"Wrapped packages. I still need to put bows on."

"Did you remember to put the presents *in* the boxes?"

"They're for decoration, not gifts. Just trust me." Hannah stepped past him into the house. "Hey Percy. Are you ready to get holidayed up?"

Percy's face lit up with something that might have been actual pleasure at the sight of her. "The tree has been soaking up water on the back porch since yesterday. The stand and everything else is in the attic."

"I cleared a path to the ladder in the garage," Ryan told her.

"Excellent. Let me just set all these down and make a stop in the kitchen. I brought cookie dough."

"Cookie dough?" That was definitely hope in the old man's voice.

"You can't decorate for Christmas without cookies and cocoa. And what's the point of being related to the baker in town if you can't filch cookie dough from the supply in the freezer?"

Ryan set down the bags beside hers in the entryway. "I like the way you think."

She switched the oven on to heat. "Okay, let's start hauling stuff down."

Percy started to shuffle into the living room. "I'll just put on my shoes."

"You're not going up that ladder." Ryan hated the mutinous turn of his expression. "You were dizzy this morning. If you fell and injured yourself, that would put a serious cramp in these decorating plans."

Percy huffed. "Fine."

"Actually, I was thinking you could hook us up with some music," Hannah suggested. "Do you have a radio or CD player?"

His lips twitched. "I expect I could manage something."

She beamed. "Wonderful. Then we'll get started bringing stuff down from the attic."

"Tree stand is in the northwest corner."

"I'm on it," Ryan promised.

He preceded Hannah up the ladder, groping around until he found the chain and tugged it. Dim light illuminated only part of the space. "Holy shit."

"What?"

In answer, he hauled himself up the rest of the way and made room for her. She poked her head through the floor. "Oh my."

"And I thought the garage was bad."

The attic was full to the brim with stuff. The detritus of forty plus years of living in the same place. Boxes, trunks, and bins were stacked neatly along the sides, with an assortment of furniture, ancient luggage, and sporting equipment that probably dated back to when Percy and Janie had been newlyweds wedged between. There was barely room to walk between the rows.

Hannah climbed up the rest of the way, taking his hand for balance when he offered. "Well, he said the tree stand is in the northwest corner. Let's start with that and hope the rest of the Christmas stuff is nearby." Whipping out her phone, she swiped on the flashlight and edged toward the front corner of the house.

"Hold up. I should probably go first. I don't know what kind of shape the floors are in. Nobody's been up here in God knows how long."

"It's fine. I'm walking along the beams."

He hurried behind her, having to turn sideways to ease between the stacks of boxes. All this stuff needed going through, too. That was likely more than he'd manage in his time here. He'd clean up and clear out the garage, fix anything that needed fixing around the house to ensure Percy's safety, and put his mother and brothers on the rest. Let them fight the battle over what needed to be donated or tossed.

"Good Lord, there must be at least sixteen boxes of decorations over here," Hannah observed. "And here's the stand."

"If you can start passing things back to me, I'll make a stack by the ladder."

They got into a rhythm, transferring boxes from one space to the next. When they filled the small area of empty floor by the ladder, they set up yet another chain so that she could pass boxes down to him on the ground. He made an effort not to watch her ass during the process, but really, it was a lost cause when she filled out those skinny jeans like a gift from God. Once they'd hauled the first lot into the foyer, they went back and repeated the process.

"Is that everything?" he asked.

She held her phone up high. "I think so. Let me just check this back row of boxes."

A sharp crack of splintering wood echoed through the attic. Even as she yelped, he leapt forward, grabbing her around the waist and hauling her back before she could plunge through the floor and the ceiling below. Her phone clattered across the plywood.

"You okay?"

"I...yeah." Her voice was level enough, but her hands had fisted in his shirt, hanging on, and her body trembled against his in the wake of the adrenaline dump.

The light from wherever her phone landed cast crazy shadows on her face as she looked up at him, her pupils blown wide, and Ryan forgot for a second that it had been a mere fall he'd saved her from. His own pulse was hammering with more than just adrenaline, and he couldn't quite stop his hands from sliding over her hips and partway up her spine to pull her closer. She licked her lips, flattening her palms against his chest.

Just one taste...

He started to close the distance between them.

"Everything okay up there?" Percy's voice echoed up from the garage, as effective as a bucket of ice water. "I thought I heard a crash."

"It's fine," Ryan called back, not taking his eyes off Hannah's. "Some of the attic flooring is rotten. I'll fix it later. Nobody's hurt."

"We'd best get to it. Lots of work to do." Flashing a wry smile, she stepped back.

The keen edge of disappointment sliced through him at another opportunity lost.

CHAPTER 6

*H*annah backed away from Ryan before she did something crazy like leap back into his arms and climb him like a tree. Scooping up her phone, she backed down the ladder, lifting her gaze to his just before her head cleared the entrance. He was still standing where she'd left him, a hungry expression in his eyes. Her cheeks heated. She ducked her head, but not before his lips curved into a smile.

Needing a chance to find her composure after the near miss of falling through the floor —sure, it was the near miss and not the near kiss—she directed Ryan and Percy outside to fit the tree into the stand while she began slicing cookies to bake.

She definitely hadn't imagined it this time. They'd been having a Moment, damn it. Ryan had been seconds away from kissing her, and then—Perseus Interruptus. Fifteen months since she'd been kissed. Longer than that since anyone had tempted her for more. She'd been fine with that until him. And now she was supposed to work alongside him decorating this house and pretend she wasn't thinking about what those muscles she'd felt beneath her hands would look like without a shirt?

Huffing out a breath, she arranged dough on the cookie sheet she'd unearthed. It would be fine. There was bound to be some other opportunity, right? And now that she knew she wasn't imagining things, she could help create an opportunity. That wasn't cheating, was it?

The guys came back inside as she was sliding the tray of cookies into the oven.

"What kind of cookies are those?" Percy

asked.

Because he sounded like a curious little boy, Hannah found a smile. "Ginger snaps. They'll make the house smell like Christmas as we decorate."

"Are you ready for me to bring the tree inside?" If Ryan was still affected by the almost kiss, it didn't show in his expression.

Fine. Two could play at that game. "Let's finish clearing the space."

Between the two of them, they shifted around living room furniture to make room in front of the big picture window, then hauled in the tree. Once the netting was cut and the branches sprang out, she directed him in making the minute adjustments necessary so that it stood straight and tall. He was a good sport through the process, lips curved in an indulgent smile. By the time she was happy with it, the buzzer was going off for the cookies.

"Ryan, can you sort the stuff in the foyer into indoor and outdoor piles, while I deal with the cookies?"

"Yes ma'am."

Hannah headed for the kitchen, trailed by her octogenarian shadow.

"If I didn't know any better, I'd say the boy was flirting," Percy observed.

"Is that an unusual state of affairs?" She pulled the cookies from the oven and began transferring them to the cooling rack she'd found earlier.

"Not his default setting. Always has his mind on the mission. That's his Delta Force training."

She bobbled a cookie. "Delta Force? He's special forces?"

"Didn't mention that, huh?"

"No." Now his reticence at dinner last night made more sense. He was a certified badass.

"He won't brag on himself, so I'll brag for him. He's a special forces medical sergeant and a damned good one."

"Mmhmm, I'm so good you won't let me examine you." Ryan's expression was clearly dialed to not amused as he joined them.

"I got all my limbs still attached and no shrapnel sticking out of me. I'm not in need of your services," Percy insisted.

Hannah caught the faint tightening in Ryan's jaw. She wanted to touch him, to soothe that stress away and make him forget about Percy's careless words.

"These cookies need a few minutes to cool," she said. "Percy, weren't you in charge of music?"

"Reckon I was. I apologize." He snatched a cookie from the rack and tossed it from hand to hand to cool as he walked out of the room.

Because she wasn't a woman who tended to ignore the urges of her heart, she crossed to Ryan and laid a hand on his arm. The muscles were corded with tension. His dark eyes fixed on hers. She didn't say anything—didn't know what *to* say—just ran her hand down his arm until her fingers could link with his. An offering of comfort. After a moment, his hand closed around hers, strong and warm.

Jazz piano spilled out from the living room.

Ryan canted his head to the side as if trying to identify the song. Hannah recognized it instantly.

"*A Charlie Brown Christmas*. The Vince Guaraldi Trio."

One corner of his mouth kicked up. "You know, like, every Christmas song ever made, don't you?"

"Maybe not *every* one, but a lot. And come on, this is a classic Christmas soundtrack. Didn't you watch *A Charlie Brown Christmas* as a kid?"

"We were much more into *A Christmas Story.*"

"That is only the worst Christmas movie ever made."

The other side of his mouth curved. "It's a classic. I mean, obviously—they have an all day marathon of it every year."

"I don't think we can be friends anymore." She called it a win when his eyes lost that haunted edge.

"Friends," he murmured. "Is that what we're

doing?"

Fresh tension snapped between them, stealing her breath. How could he turn the mood so fast?

"You two comin'?" Percy shouted.

Something hot flickered in Ryan's gaze.

Oh, mercy. Finding her voice, Hannah managed to call back, "Just plating the cookies!" With one last squeeze of Ryan's hand, she moved to make up a tray with still warm cookies and glasses of milk for everybody. Maybe the milk would cool the heat in her cheeks.

The music, as it turned out, was from a fabulous vintage turntable and speakers. "I bought this system forty years ago. Spent a pretty penny. The speakers alone cost the earth." Percy named a figure that had her wincing, even now. "Thought my Janie was gonna kill me dead. But she loved music and it was something we enjoyed together."

"It sounds amazing. There's nothing like real vinyl. It's...I don't know...warmer somehow."

"I haven't listened to these in a long time," Percy admitted. "My Janie, she used to have music on all the time. While she cooked or cleaned. Even while she gardened. She'd open the windows and play it loud enough half the street could hear. Thankfully the neighbors appreciated our taste in music."

Hannah laughed and began to open boxes. "That's fortunate."

"Her favorite thing, though, was to put on something romantic after dinner and dance. She was a helluva dancer. I never could do much but sway and instigate the occasional spin, but she never minded."

The image he painted warmed her heart even as it made her ache for what he'd lost. What would it be like to have fifty years like that with someone you loved? Perilously close to tears, she turned to the business of things, tasking Ryan with untangling twinkle lights while she took inventory of what they had to work with.

Percy helped her unpack things, telling stories about this ornament or that. In every word, every look, it was clear he adored his wife and missed her like a limb. For a while, she worried that all the memories would send him spiraling into grief. But each little anecdote, each new record, seemed to coax out a smile.

"You remind me of her, with all that holiday cheer. Not even a grumpy old cuss like me can resist."

She couldn't think of a higher compliment. As the latest album shifted into Frank Sinatra's rendition of "The Christmas Song", she put down the box of painted glass balls and held out a hand. "Will you dance with me, Percy?"

His wrinkled cheeks pinked and he began to bluster.

"Please?"

"Well. All right." He set aside the ornaments in his hands and curled his fingers around hers, settling his other hand lightly on her waist.

As they began to circle to the music, awareness skated over her skin from the weight of Ryan's gaze. She couldn't help but wonder what it would be like to dance with him, with that battled-hardened body pressed to hers, staring into those eyes that seemed to see straight into her soul.

Needing a distraction, she focused on her actual dance partner. "How did you meet your Janie, Percy?"

"We met because of another woman."

"Oh reeeeeally?" She drew the word out to three syllables. "It sounds like there's a story there."

"I had a date with her roommate. A buddy of mine set us up. She was the sister or cousin of somebody or other—I forget. Anyway, she shared a house with four other gals, and she wasn't ready when I got there to pick her up. So I was sitting there in the living room, cooling my heels when Janie walks in. Prettiest thing I ever saw. I had no idea she wasn't my date. She just said, 'You ready?' And all I could do was nod because I didn't have control over my tongue."

"Wait, wait. You took Janie out instead of

your actual date?" Hannah asked.

"I did. And we had a grand old time. She didn't fess up until *after* I'd brought her home. I was leaning in to kiss her goodnight and the door flies open and there's Bridget, madder than a wet hen."

"Bet that was awkward," Ryan observed.

"I didn't know what to say. Janie just shrugged and said we wouldn't have had anything in common anyway and she was just saving us both from a miserable evening. Bridget slammed the door on us and locked it. That was about the time Janie realized she didn't have her key. We ended up sitting on the front porch, talking until the sun came up, and by the end of that night, I knew I was gonna marry that girl—which I did a year later."

The story left Hannah's heart warm and gooey. "Insult to Bridget aside, that's so romantic."

"When you know, you know," Percy said simply, dropping his hands as the music ended. "Thank you for the dance, young lady."

"Thank you for the story." She smiled at him and picked up a set of handmade ornaments of the three wise men. "Now tell me about these."

As afternoon wore into evening, Ryan watched Hannah continue to work her magic on the house and on Percy himself. She drew him out, reminding him of all the good memories attached to this stuff. Percy seemed to get five years younger in as many hours as she continued chattering away like a cheerful magpie. She was so *open* and willing to connect with everyone around her. His hand flexed at the remembered feel of her fingers laced through his. He couldn't fathom being like that, being able to *survive* like that. And she seemed to thrive on it. It fascinated him. She fascinated him, despite his better judgment, and he couldn't help but wonder what she'd do if Percy wasn't around to interrupt.

As if reading his mind, Percy shoved up

from the recliner. "I hate to leave good company, but I'm tuckered out."

He didn't look over-tired. Their efforts had put color in his cheeks and a spring in his step. Or maybe he was as hopped up on sugar as a third grader who'd cleaned out the cookie jar. His hands shook a little. Either way, it was getting close to his bedtime.

Hannah glanced around at the chaos of the living room, a frown bowing that pretty mouth. "I'm so sorry. I didn't expect this to take so long."

Percy waved a hand. "I should've warned you. Decorating was a multi-day affair with my Janie. It'll still be here tomorrow. And there's still the outside to finish."

Which meant she'd be back. Ryan didn't care to analyze the sudden surge of relief.

"I'll just finish up with the tree and get out of your hair for the night."

"Don't rush on my account." Percy turned toward the stairs, shooting a wink in Ryan's direction.

The back of his neck heated. Was he that transparent? He prided himself on being able to keep his emotions under control. But sweet, unassuming Hannah Wheeler was getting under his skin.

She bit her lip and he tried not to stare. "I didn't mean to wear him out."

"I think he's had more fun today than he has in years. This was good for him." Tearing his gaze away from her mouth, Ryan started clearing away the empty boxes.

"Maybe I should just wait to finish the rest of this tomorrow."

He ought to agree. To let her go, so he could get himself back under control. "Do you have the early shift again?"

"No. Late shift. I don't go in until two."

"Then stay." So much for control.

She stood across the room, but he could read the pleasure, the interest in her gaze.

Yeah, he wasn't the only one remembering that interrupted moment in the attic.

Pursuing this wasn't smart. It wasn't what she deserved. But maybe they both needed to address the attraction between them. To answer that *what if?* At least, he hoped that's what she wanted.

"Okay."

Unlike with Percy, she didn't keep up a running commentary as she continued to work, slipping instead into silence. But it wasn't an awkward quiet. While he cleaned up, she made garland for the mantle and around the door from fresh evergreen boughs. The brightly wrapped packages she'd brought became their own form of garland over some of the windows. It should've looked weird but was actually pretty amazing. Bright and happy, like something out of Santa's workshop. By the time they were down to the last box, the house had been transformed into a winter wonderland. Janie's nutcrackers were nestled around the house with ribbon and greenery, and the Christmas village he remembered from his childhood was displayed in a place of honor on the far side of the den. Every room held the touch and scent of the holidays.

"Not bad, Miss Wheeler. Not bad at all."

Her lips curved in satisfaction as she surveyed her handiwork. "It did come out pretty well, if I do say so myself."

"Is there some official celebration of a finished tree?"

Her dimples flashed. "As it happens, there is. I'll make the hot chocolate."

He didn't follow her into the kitchen. Instead, he dug through Percy's record collection, wanting more music as a backdrop to whatever was left of their evening. She came back a few minutes later, as he was slipping another album on the turntable.

"It's too hot to drink yet, but I added extra marshmallows. Hope you don't mind."

"I feel like extra marshmallows on hot chocolate is a rule."

She grinned. "Now you're catching on."

Music began to spill quietly from the speakers. Jazz piano gave way to the familiar, moody brass of Miles Davis. Ryan held out a hand. "Will you dance with me?"

Surprise flashed across her face. But she hesitated only a moment before setting the mugs down and placing her hand in his. He pulled her in, settling his hand at the small of her back as her arm curved around his shoulder, her fingers just brushing his nape. A shiver of arousal worked its way down his spine. He liked how she fit in his arms, liked the easy way her body curved into his. He liked pretty much everything about this woman.

"Thank you for doing this for my uncle. It definitely seems to have improved his spirits."

She tipped her head. "What about yours?"

The question seemed serious rather than flirty, so he answered honestly. "I concede my spirits are lifted, too." And wasn't that a surprise? He hadn't even been aware they needed lifting. Maybe the job was wearing on him more than he'd realized.

"Then I'd say my mission has been a success."

"Is that what this is for you? A mission? Operation Christmas?" The idea of it had a mental image unfolding in his brain of her in some kind of camo elf uniform, marching through the base to pass out cookies and holiday cheer. That'd be a helluva thing to see.

"Percy was my mission. You're…something else."

He circled them in the glow of the twinkle lights, considering his words. "I'm probably a bad idea."

"Why?"

"I'm only here for a little while. I'll be back overseas before you can blink, and I won't be home again for—honestly, I don't know how long. My deployment means I'm often out of contact for days or weeks at a time. I'm not in any kind of position to start something."

"Which one of us are you trying to convince?"

He huffed a soft laugh. "I'm just saying, I know this isn't ideal." And there was the out if she wanted it.

Her eyes didn't stray from his. "But?" The hopeful note had his fingers flexing against her.

He searched her face, not finding any reluctance or concern. "But if I don't kiss you, I think it's going to haunt me, wondering what you taste like."

She shifted closer, her hand curling around his nape and stroking the fine hair there until he wanted to purr like some giant cat. "I'd say you have enough ghosts without adding that to the mix."

Hallelujah.

He bent his head until it was just a whisper away from hers and held there, right at the edge of temptation.

She pulled back a fraction. "What are you waiting for?" she whispered.

"Percy's interruption."

It was her turn to laugh. "He has had pretty crap timing today. But I think he's really gone to bed. And if he hasn't, he's invested enough in his matchmaking effort to stay out of the way."

"Caught that, did you?"

"He's not subtle."

Ryan winced. "Sorry about that."

"I think it's sweet."

"Sweet is not the word I'd use."

"Ryan?" Amusement glittered in those big blue eyes.

"Yeah?"

"Stop thinking." To make sure he did, she rose to her toes and touched her lips to his.

His mind emptied of everything but her. He'd imagined she'd be tentative, with a soft mouth ready to be coaxed. But she kissed like she did everything else—with a sweet enthusiasm. She *was* soft in all the best ways, pliant and willing as he wrapped her tighter in his arms and better angled his head to taste her. He traced the seam of her lips with his tongue and she opened for him with a sexy little moan that shot his body temperature up. She tasted of gingerbread, sweet and a little spicy. He wondered if she'd be like that in bed.

When he caught himself calculating the distance to the sofa, he tugged hard on the reins of his control. They weren't alone in this house and that was a lot further than he'd meant to go. Ruthlessly throttling his arousal, he gentled the kiss, sifting his fingers through the silk of her hair to stroke down her back. She arched into the touch, fraying his hard-won control. When he could manage it, he set them swaying again to whatever new song played and eased back just enough to rest his brow against hers.

"Did that satisfy your curiosity?" Her breathless voice had a whole host of other needs rearing up and demanding satisfaction.

"I'm pretty sure that was a potato chip kiss."

"A what?"

"You know that whole tagline? You can't have just one."

A delighted giggle burbled out of her, and it was the cutest damned thing. "You won't hear me complaining."

As the music shifted yet again, she relaxed into him, settling her head against his shoulder with a sigh. A quiet contentment seeped through him. It had been so long since the rest of his ghosts were quiet. That was a seduction of itself, whether she meant it to be or not. Was this what Percy had felt dancing with Janie after dinner? It would be easy, *so* very easy to fall into the appeal of this woman. To pretend he had more time, more…everything to give her. But he didn't. And he could already tell that walking away from her was going to be harder than he'd imagined. His hands tightened around her.

"Hannah—"

"What did I say about thinking?"

"I know but—"

She pulled back enough to meet his gaze and cupped his cheek. "You were clear about the boundaries of this, and I'm still here. I like you, and you like me. Can't we just roll with that?"

It wasn't in his nature or training to simply accept things as they came. Everything in his life was carefully planned, with contingency plans and protocols for when things went off the rails. He survived by always considering the possible outcomes and alternatives. Looking ten steps ahead but being ready for a disaster to come out of nowhere anyway. Every single variation he could think of where he actively pursued things with Hannah ended the same way—with one or both of them hurt when he went back to war. Was it worth taking what she was offering when that was the consequence?

She brushed her lips over his again. "I don't know what's going on with my life, either. Let's just...spend some time together while you're here. Enjoy each other. Whatever that looks like. Don't over complicate it."

Damn Percy for putting his brain on this path.

Ryan pulled her close. "You have no idea how much I want to say yes to that offer. But I still have a job to do here. I need to be able to make recommendations for Percy when I go, and he's not showing any signs of being willing to cooperate."

"He's willing to cooperate for me."

"You think you can sweet talk him into getting a proper physical from the doctor?"

"Probably not. But I *can* help talk him into activities that would enable you to check him out."

The idea intrigued him. "Like what?

"There's a Christmas dance out at Applewhite Farms on Friday night. We could go. It'd be a chance to see him in a social setting, get him out of the house. I guarantee his isolation is a huge part of his issue. I'm pretty sure Percy's benefactor will be there. We could try to nudge them together. And we've already established he'll dance with me. You can get a better gauge of his physical capabilities." Her lips curved. "And hopefully you'll save a few dances for me yourself."

It wasn't a half-bad idea. He had no idea what a small town dance consisted of, but at this point, he'd follow her just about anywhere to keep soaking up the warmth of that smile. "Then I'd say we have a date."

CHAPTER 7

"I don't know why you dragged me out with you tonight," Percy grumped. "In my day we didn't want chaperones on a date."

Hannah tucked her arm more firmly in his, both as a means of keeping him from turning back to the truck and to help him navigate the uneven terrain of the gravel drive up to the big barn of Applewhite Farms.

Ryan trailed a pace behind, on Percy's other side, ready to steady him if he stumbled. "We don't need a chaperone."

"Then you're doing this date thing all wrong."

She snorted with laughter and popped him lightly on the arm. "Percy!"

"Well, you are," he insisted, but a smile hovered at the edge of his thin lips as he glanced over at her.

She grinned back, buoyed by his improved mood. "Unsolicited advice on how a date should work aside, you're here because the Merry Mingle is a good cause. Proceeds go toward building a proper play area in the children's wing at the hospital. You know you want to make sure those kids have something more than second-hand board games. Besides, it'll be fun. Where's your holiday spirit?"

"I spent it all on decorating the house. Who's gonna put all that stuff away when Christmas is over?"

She started to say that she and Ryan would, then remembered he'd be gone by then. As that fell firmly into the category of do-not-want-to-think-about, Hannah fixed her smile in place. "I will." She'd get Omar to help with the bigger boxes. Nudging her shoulder gently against Percy's, she insisted, "No excuses. We're here to have fun tonight, and you're gonna save me some dances."

Evan Applewhite, Jace's dad, manned the door selling tickets. "Welcome, welcome! How many?"

"Three, please," Ryan told him. He paid the man and the three of them stepped into a whirl of light and music.

Applewhite Farms was *the* Christmas destination in Wishful. Not only did they supply most of the fresh Christmas trees in town, they also knew how to throw a serious holiday party. A band was set up at one end of the big barn and fat Christmas lights crisscrossed the space above them, combined with lots of greenery and ribbon to provide a festive air. A good hundred people milled through the building, rocking out to "Run, Run Rudolph" or hovering around one of the tables at the edges. A cash bar was set up in one corner, and a refreshment table took up another.

"Percy Gannaway! We haven't seen you for a coon's age!" Delia Watson's voice boomed above the music.

If she hadn't been holding his arm, Hannah wouldn't have noticed the momentary tensing of his muscles as the Casserole Patrol wandered over.

"Evenin', ladies."

"And who is this handsome young man?" Maudie Bell asked, giving Ryan the once over.

"My nephew, Sergeant Ryan Malone." He made introductions.

Ryan inclined his head, with a very proper "Ma'am" for each of them. A trio of identical blushes stained their cheeks.

"I drove by your house the other day. It looks amazing," Maudie Bell gushed. "It's good to see you getting back into the Christmas spirit."

Percy jerked his shoulders. "Seemed like it was time."

"Hannah's work?" Delia asked.

"Yes, ma'am," Hannah confirmed.

Maudie Bell swatted Betty on the arm. "You were absolutely right to send her over there."

Percy shot a surprised glance in Betty's direction. "This was your idea?"

Betty shrugged, a hotter blush staining her cheeks. "I thought you'd enjoy it."

Definite crush.

"Well." He stopped there until Hannah nudged him in the ribs. "Thank you."

Chester Harkin, Maudie Bell's live-in beau, walked up with drinks in hand. "Percy."

"Chester."

"House looks great. You're giving my Maudie Bell ideas."

Maudie Bell practically cackled. "I had ideas well before now. But I think I will have Hannah come by to spruce things up before the kids come."

"I'd be happy to," Hannah said.

Ryan slipped his hand in hers. "If you'll excuse us, I think we're going to go dance."

Percy waved them off. "Go, go. Have fun."

As Ryan towed her away, Percy asked the others, "Y'all doing okay?"

"Can't complain, can't complain. When are you gonna come down to the senior center for bingo night?" Delia demanded.

"Oh, leave the man alone," Betty insisted. "You know he hates bingo."

The rest of their conversation got swallowed up by the music.

The band shifted into a rendition of "Let It Snow". As Ryan pulled her into his arms, Hannah's gaze lingered on Percy.

"Relax, he's fine," Ryan murmured.

"But what if he needs a rescue?"

"We made him come out tonight so he'd socialize. You have to give him a chance to do that."

She bit her lip. "I know. It's just…I've gotten attached to him over the past few days. What if this is too much for him?"

"These are his lifelong friends. He's okay. See, he's asked Betty to dance." Ryan circled them so she had a clear view of Percy leading Betty onto the floor.

"He seems to have taken her gesture well. You think he's ready to think about maybe dating again?"

"Your guess is as good as mine. He about ripped me a new one when I brought it up the other day. But enough about Percy, for now. I'm more interested in you." Ryan lost some of that sober expression that seemed to be his default, a smile crinkling the corners of his eyes as he pulled her closer.

"Well, that's sure nice to hear." She snuggled in, reveling the press of his body against hers.

As they swayed to the music, everything else faded to the background, until she couldn't think of anything but him. His big, broad hand splayed against the small of her back, fingers kneading slightly, as if he wished he were touching skin. She found herself mimicking the motion against the back of his neck and enjoyed watching his pupils spring wide.

Knowing she affected him was as heady and intoxicating as her grandmother's eggnog.

"How do you feel about traditions?" he asked.

"Generally a big fan. Why?"

"Because we're standing under mistletoe."

She glanced up and spotted the kissing ball dangling over their heads. "It's bad luck not to kiss under mistletoe."

"Can't be having any of that," he murmured, his eyes full of affection and heat.

"Definitely not," she agreed, already breathless.

His mouth brushed over hers, and she sighed, melting into him. This was dangerous. Oh, so dangerous. It could become an addiction. *He* could become an addiction. But she couldn't make herself pull back, couldn't make herself look beyond what he made her feel in the moment.

By the time he eased back, resting his brow against hers, the song had changed.

"You're exceptionally good at that,

Sergeant."

Ryan huffed a laugh and brushed a kiss to her temple before resting his cheek there with a sigh she hoped was contentment.

"I have a question." His voice was a delicious rumble.

Please let it be when can we get out of here. "I expect I can probably come up with an answer."

"Your year ban on driving was up a couple months ago. Have you driven at all since then?"

All her relaxed arousal evaporated in an instant. She didn't want to talk about this, didn't want one more person she had to defend her actions to. Sucking in a breath, she put some distance between them. "Why?"

"Just curious."

Given what she'd told him on their date, of course he'd wondered. And of course he'd asked. There was no reason to treat the topic like it was a state secret, and nothing in his expression suggested he thought she was crazy or stupid or any of the other things she'd felt herself over the past two months as she'd wrestled with it.

"No, I haven't driven."

"Why?"

Carolanne had been circling around this question in her unobtrusive therapist way for weeks. Something about Ryan's directness compelled her to answer honestly.

"I'm actually terrified to drive." She winced at the admission. "That must sound incredibly stupid to someone in your profession."

"There are all kinds of fears, none of them stupid to the person who has them."

"That's kind of you to say."

"Not kindness. Just the truth. Is it that you're afraid of having another seizure?"

A rational conclusion, but not the right one. "I'm afraid of hurting somebody else. It was a minor miracle nobody but me was hurt or killed last time. No one's that lucky twice."

"Is that why you're staying in Wishful?"

"Partly." No reason to deny it. The small town meant less opportunity for disaster. "But beyond that, I like Wishful. I like the pace and the people here. And I've decided to apply to the small business incubator to see if I can start my own firm." It was the first time she'd admitted it aloud since she'd made the decision. She hadn't been able to bring herself to tell Carolanne. Somehow Ryan was an easier audience. He wasn't invested in the outcome.

Interest lit his dark eyes. "Yeah? How's that work?"

"Basically it's like a little business nest. Lots of little start ups in one place, sharing overhead and workspace and resources. And there's a mentorship component that really appeals to me. I understand the design aspect of my work without problem. I don't need leadership there. But the business side is a whole other story. This feels like the best of both worlds. I can do things on my terms. That appeals to me a lot more than going back to a big city firm with all the backbiting and competition."

"That makes sense. But surely your future

client-base would go beyond here. Won't you need to drive for that?"

The question was all practicality, so she fought not to bristle, but she really wanted him to drop the issue. "Yes. And I'll get there. I'm just...not ready yet."

She waited for him to argue with her or offer to drive with her to get her over the hump, but he simply nodded, accepting. Something in her relaxed. He wasn't going to push or judge. And why should he? This thing between them was temporary. Whether she drove or not didn't affect him long-term. If that gave her more than a little pang, Hannah ignored it. She just wanted to focus on the right here and now.

The music came to an end and they broke apart, applauding.

"Holy shit," Ryan murmured.

"What?" Hannah followed his gaze to see Percy and Betty caught under one of the many mistletoe kissing balls hanging around the space. "Oh man, how's he going to get out of this?"

"Looks like he's not."

As they watched, Percy bent and pressed a light kiss to Betty's lips. It wasn't lengthy or particularly demonstrative, and he pulled back almost immediately, stunned surprise lighting his face. But he didn't let her go or walk away.

"Well," Ryan said. "This is gonna be interesting."

"IF THE MILITARY ever decides to go with a softer touch, they could learn a thing or two from you."

Hannah just shot Ryan a secretive smile as they followed Brooke Redding, director of the Wishful Animal Rescue, down the central aisle between kennels as dogs barked, bayed, and whined from all sides. He had no idea how she'd managed to convince Percy to volunteer for dog walking duty, and he'd been standing right there. It was something to do with those big blue eyes and the dimples. He wasn't exactly immune to that combination himself. Either way, this latest scheme to help him covertly assess Percy's physical health was a good one.

"—so appreciate y'all coming down. We're always in need of something down here. Volunteers, supplies, donations. With the holiday season and winter finally getting started, we're even shorter than usual on all of the above," Brooke explained. "I'm trying to do a big push to clear out most of the animals before the real cold hits. We aren't equipped for any serious winter weather."

Most of the facilities were outside, under aluminum awnings. Rather than proper walls, a series of tarps were stretched to help block the wind. It wasn't a bad setup for mild weather, but if they had a freak cold snap below freezing, the rigged space would be seriously problematic. They needed a real building.

"I've been running an adoption special to try to encourage people to gift a shelter animal for Christmas," Brooke continued. "Several of our puppies and kittens have been picked up from that promotion, but that leaves our older animals."

"Poor babies," Hannah cooed. "Who's in need of some love?"

Ryan considered raising his hand.

Brooke stopped in front of a kennel where a mutt that had to be mostly shepherd lay on a raised bed in the corner. "This is Duke."

He didn't even lift his head.

"He was surrendered this summer after his owner passed. Her kids didn't want to take him, so they brought him here. He's older. About nine years, so people keep skipping over him for younger dogs. Poor guy's just gotten more and more depressed."

That was a familiar story. Ryan glanced at Percy to see if the tale upset him at all. His uncle's face was full of disgust rather than discomfort. He definitely eyed the animal with sympathy.

"Well no wonder." Hannah crouched in front of the chainlink, curling her fingers through the wire. "Hey Duke. Hey buddy. You want some exercise?" she crooned.

His ears twitched.

"How is he on lead?" she asked.

"A perfect gentleman," Brooke said. "He's really well trained, fully housebroken. He just doesn't get on in a household with multiple pets, so that's also made him harder to place. Either way, some exercise would do him good."

"How about it, Percy? You want to take this guy around the yard a bit?"

"I expect so."

Brooke opened the gate and moved inside to slip on a leash and collar. She made clucking noises. "C'mon, Duke."

With a fair amount of grumbling that reminded Ryan of Percy himself, the dog rose and stretched before plodding obediently out of the kennel. When Brooke handed over the leash, Duke sat with a sigh and eyed Percy as if to say, "So you're the next in the line of disappointments, huh?" Percy let the dog sniff his hand before giving him a scratch behind the ears.

"Reckon we could both do with a little exercise. Let's go."

Duke rose to his feet and followed Percy out the gate at the end of the corridor and into the exercise yard.

"Are you sure this is a good idea?" Ryan muttered to Hannah.

"Just give it a little time. Those two have more than a little in common."

"That did not escape my notice." He pinned Hannah with a Look. "What are you up to?"

Her face was all innocence. "I told you. Getting him some exercise and helping you evaluate him."

He might have believed her if she and Brooke hadn't exchanged some kind of secret glance. "You're hoping he falls in love and takes him home."

Brooke pressed her lips together, eyes sparkling. "I'm just gonna let you two discuss. There are leashes on the wall over there. Grab whoever you want for a walk."

As soon as she walked away, Hannah turned

toward him, hands on hips, brows up. "And what if I am?"

"That's a terrible idea. If he ends up needing to go into assisted living, where would that leave an animal? That poor dog has been through enough."

"I get your concerns. Really, I do. But think about it. Percy let himself decline after Janie died because he no longer had anybody to take care of, and so he didn't have any impetus to take care of himself. If he got a dog, he'd have another creature depending on him again. One that would require regular exercise and attention, *both* of which would do Percy good himself. Dogs are a lot of company, and I think he needs that."

"And if he adopts an older one like Duke and then outlives the dog? What then?" Losing Janie had gutted Percy. If he opened himself up again, let himself get attached, and then lost the dog, would it make him shut down again?

She angled her head, and those big, blue

eyes seemed to look into him. "Did you have a dog growing up?"

"Trixie. Big old sloppy black lab. She died when I was a sophomore in college. Made it to sixteen. Broke my heart." He was man enough to admit that.

"Did you ever get another dog?"

"No. I knew I was going into the Army when I finished school. Didn't make sense to get another one for that short stint."

"So you haven't connected with any other dog since then?"

Ryan shrugged. "It wasn't practical. We've got some technically illegal dogs on base that we all share responsibility for, but I haven't had my own dog since I was a kid." He hadn't been willing to risk it.

"I think it scares you."

The accusation had his head kicking back. "Excuse me?"

"The idea of letting yourself get attached to something like that again, knowing you'll eventually lose it—that scares you. You think it's easier to avoid attachment in the first place."

Were they still talking about dogs? Or had this gone on into something else?

"I deal with loss on an almost daily basis." And if he'd had to learn to shut down the part of himself that cared, well, that was a matter of survival.

"Dealing with it isn't the same as not being afraid of it. Loss sucks. Grief sucks. But it's a part of life. And I don't think it overshadows the payoff of the attachment in the first place." Hannah curled her hands in his, her expression full of such warmth and understanding, he almost wanted to take a step back. Because that part he'd worked so damned hard to shut down had been stirring back to life since she'd walked into his.

"Sorry I'm late!"

He lifted his head to find Miss Betty hurrying down the corridor. "Late?"

Hannah released him and approached the

older woman with a smile. "I'll just get Coco on a leash for you."

"Coco?" Ryan asked.

"Oh yes, Coco and I have a regular walking date three times a week," Miss Betty informed him.

"And how do you know Coco?" he asked, as Hannah disappeared into one of the other kennels with a leash.

"I might volunteer down here on a regular basis," she called back.

"Uh huh." He watched as she led some little poodle mix out and handed it over to Miss Betty.

"Percy's already out in the yard with Duke. They might appreciate some company."

Miss Betty beamed and hurried on outside with her charge.

Ryan stared after her, then turned to Hannah. "You are a sneaky, sneaky woman."

"Well, he *did* kiss her at the dance."

"I can't decide if you're brilliant or terrifying."

She grinned. "I can be both. Now pick your pooch. We're here to work *while* we matchmake."

In honor of Trixie, Ryan leashed up a young lab mix aptly dubbed Pogo. The dog did more bouncing than walking as they made their way out to the yard with Hannah and her chosen companion, a border collie mix named Dolly. They spent twenty minutes walking and chatting, working with the dogs on their leash manners. Brooke wandered out with a tennis ball and suggested some off-leash time. Pogo trembled with excitement at the sight of it and Dolly bowed, butt wagging.

"How can you say no to those faces?" Hannah asked.

Across the fenced yard, Percy sat on a bench beside Miss Betty. Coco curled up in her lap and Duke stretched out at their feet, not remotely enticed by the idea of a game.

Ryan unclipped the leash from Pogo's collar, pausing to give the dog a full body rubdown. "Wanna play? Huh? You want the ball?"

Pogo barked, leaping up to slobber a cheerful kiss across Ryan's face.

He wiped it with his sleeve. "I'll take that as a yes."

Accepting the ball from Brooke, he winged it to the far end of the yard. Pogo and Dolly tore after it, feet scrambling, muscles bunching as they streaked across the brown grass. It was such a simple thing, playing fetch with a dog. Repetitive. It should've been boring. But watching the unfettered joy of the animals as they chased after the little yellow sphere was oddly soothing. Hannah had talked a lot this week about the idea of living in the present. It was hard to get any more present than this. It was pleasure he hadn't known he'd missed, and he found himself grateful for Hannah's machinations for his sake, as well as Percy's. From time to time, he glanced over at his uncle, noticing that Duke had shifted close enough that Percy could periodically scratch his ears.

Nearly an hour later, Pogo and Dolly dropped down to their bellies, tongues lolling, sides heaving as they panted. Their eyes were bright and happy. Ryan himself was more relaxed than he could remember being in ages.

Percy and Betty were still hanging out on the bench, watching the show. Duke was resting his head on Percy's feet.

"You've made a friend there, I think," Ryan observed.

"I'm taking him home with me," Percy announced.

Not in the least bit surprised, he simply nodded. "Of course you are. I'll let Brooke know to start on the paperwork."

CHAPTER 8

"I love how Percy gets a dog, and somehow we're the ones home with Duke while he's out on a date with Miss Betty."

"Oh, don't be a grump." Hannah hip-checked Ryan as she moved Percy's usual massive collection of empty glasses to the sink so Ryan could set down the groceries he'd taken from her at the door. "Would you rather I be dragging you caroling tonight? Because that's still on the table." She made to abandon the food and headed for the door. "If we leave right now—"

He darted in to cut her off, using his bigger body to box her in against the counter. "I do not want to go caroling," he ground out. But it was a sexy growl, and when she tilted her head back to look up at him, his expression held both humor and heat.

Hannah felt an answering heat wash through her, felt the warmth radiating from the broad, hard body just inches away from hers. It soaked into her hands, which had settled at his waist of their own volition, igniting little fires along her skin and scrambling her brain. She widened her eyes in mock innocence and blinked up at him, fighting to keep her voice light and flirty. "Oh yeah? And what do you want to do?"

"What I want..." he rumbled low, and she could practically feel his voice. He edged in, keeping his hands on the counter behind them, until they were pressed chest to chest, hip to hip, and *oh, dear Lord* did that feel good. "What I want is to stay in and take advantage of this empty house."

"What's stopping you?" she asked, breathless, tipping her head and angling her mouth toward his.

"I didn't expect to have a four-legged chaperone."

Hannah cut her glance to where Duke was sprawled on the kitchen rug regarding them with steady brown eyes. Was he really bothered by the dog? Her lips quirked up. "Are you afraid he'll be reporting back to Percy on our shenanigans?"

"I mean, look at that face. Doesn't he seem like he's judging us?"

The dog grumbled, as if to answer the question.

"See?"

Laughing, she shoved playfully at Ryan's chest, which was about like pushing at a brick wall. "If you're concerned about reports of immodest behavior getting back to Percy, I'll restrain myself from ravishing you and feed you dinner instead."

At the word "dinner," Duke's ears pricked.

"Somebody's still hungry," she laughed.

"Wait, let's not get sidetracked. Did you just say you were going to ravish me?"

"What? Duke, did you hear me say that?" Duke swiped a paw down his muzzle. "Duke said all he heard was dinner, so I guess that's the program now."

"You," Ryan said, pointing a finger at the dog, "are a lousy wingman. What are we having?"

"Chili."

"Which needs time to simmer, right?" One corner of his mouth curved. She wanted to nibble just there, and work her way along that strong jaw.

The food wasn't the only thing at a simmer.

"It does." She slipped away from him to dig into the bags on the counter and catch her breath.

"During which time we could discuss..." He followed, moving up behind her, his chest to her shoulders, leaning down to her ear. "—dessert options."

"I do love me some dessert." The high, breathy quality of her voice wasn't a surprise. He would know exactly how he affected her, and she found she didn't mind at all.

"I'm a fan of dessert first, as it happens. *Carpe diem* and all that."

"While I am interested in your philosophies on seizing...things," she turned around, took his hands, and slapped an onion into each palm. "Good things come to those who chop."

He laughed as he backed up towards the knife block on the nearby counter. "Is that so?"

"Dice and find out."

"You're on."

The drag and thunk of a knife against butcher block was a steady beat behind her as she began to brown the ground beef. The weight of his eyes settled on her back as he chopped, and with it came the first skittering of nerves. Some of it was anticipation, but despite how much she enjoyed him, and what was happening between them, some of it was uncertainty.

Their alone time together had been limited. He was Percy's guest, and she felt weird having him over with any romantic intentions when Carolanne could walk in at any moment. So far, their escalating attraction had been limited to a lot of simmering glances, subtle flirtations, and a few toe-curling kisses. But this thing they were talking around, this dessert, that was the next level. A big step that couldn't be taken back.

What would it do to her when he left? Because he *would* leave. He'd been transparent about that from the start. He couldn't offer her what she was beginning to want with him—a long-term exploration of this connection between them. She'd never had a no-strings affair before, and she wasn't at all sure she'd survive one. Sliding over the line into love with him would be so very easy, and that was enough to make her hesitate, despite how much she wanted him.

And she did want him. That wasn't in question. She liked him, and she more than liked the kind of man he was—one who gave up his precious leave time to come help a man he considered family. But much as she'd said they should take what they could get while they could get it, she'd be lying if she didn't admit she was already attached. Maybe too attached. Crossing this line with him would only make that worse. It was how she was built.

And yet, she wanted that connection with him, and she thought he needed it with her—at least for now. Over the past week, he'd been slowly emerging from that hardened shell, letting down some of those walls. She wanted to know the man on the other side.

"You're thinking awfully hard over there."

"Guilty." She looked up and caught Ryan's grin, and somehow, that helped her find her balance again. "How do you feel about heat?"

"Honey, I am all about heat."

She smiled as she scooped up the peppers and jalapeños she'd just washed and set them down by his cutting board. "Good. Chop all of these, too."

"She's a slave driver," Ryan told Duke. He looked back at her. "He's totally judging you."

"He's judging you. He's in awe of me."

"Hannah, we're all in awe of you." Suddenly his expression was way too serious, sucking all the air out of the kitchen. "Are you thinking about your application? Because you shouldn't be nervous about that. You have amazing talent and drive."

She felt pleasant heat rise in her cheeks at his words. "I turned that in yesterday."

"Yeah? That's awesome. So if not that, what are you pondering so deeply?"

She could lie, but even the little white kind wasn't in her nature. So she shrugged. "Us. This —" She waved a hand between them, encompassing all the flirtation and innuendo and… more. "—thing."

He paused, then nodded. "What was it you've been telling me all week? Focus on the now instead of the past or too far into the future?" Despite the teasing edge to his smile, something more serious lingered beneath.

"You've done a pretty epic job keeping my mind in the here and now, and that's not easy."

"I'll take that as a compliment."

"How'd you end up that way? All cheerful Zen or whatever?"

Scooping out the browned meat with a slotted spoon, Hannah considered the question. "I focus on the now because I'm grateful to have the now, when things could've gone a whole other way in the accident. And I take pleasure and joy in the life I have, not the life I thought I'd have, or that might be just around the corner. Which isn't to say I don't plan for the future, but that's a lot hazier to me than it used to be."

Shouldn't that be her answer, then? To take the pleasure he offered and enjoy it for what it was, regardless of where it couldn't go?

"I always figured I'd be career military." With the flat of the knife, Ryan scraped the chopped vegetables into the popping grease of the pot. "That's hazier than it used to be."

"You're rethinking that path?"

"I wasn't until I came here."

Emotions like pebbles clogged her throat, each one inscribed with a wish she had for the two of them. Wishes that couldn't be voiced. She hadn't expected this from him, hadn't believed she'd really convince him he wanted or needed anything beyond this temporary, casual...thing for the holidays. She hadn't expected to want more than that herself. But there was nothing casual in his expression, nothing casual in the pulse that kicked to a gallop in her throat. The air went thick between them, and she was almost afraid to speak for fear of breaking the spell.

He skimmed his fingers through her hair. "You make me remember what I'm fighting for."

"What's that?"

He smiled a little. "Life, liberty, and the pursuit of happiness with a woman and a big, sloppy dog."

Behind them, Duke's tail thumped. Neither of them looked his way.

"Had you forgotten?" she murmured.

"I'd just...given up the wanting of them for myself. But this week with you reminded me that there's life outside war."

"Good. I wanted that for you."

"What do you want for yourself?"

Hannah blinked at him. "I..." How was she supposed to answer that? Right now, she couldn't see past this moment, past wanting him, his body against hers. And maybe that life with the big, sloppy dog. But how could she say that?

"You don't even know how to answer that, do you? You spend all this time thinking about what everybody else needs and none about yourself." He stroked a knuckle across her cheek, a whisper of a touch that scrambled her brain.

"Is there something wrong with that?"

"No. But since you're short on ideas, should I tell you what I want for you?"

"Please." She didn't know where he was going with this, but as long as he kept talking, he'd keep standing right there, close to her, with his deep, rich voice skating over her skin. She could live in this delicious moment, and not make big choices.

"In the grand scheme of things, I want you to have a career doing the thing you love, in a way that makes you happy. I want you to get to a point where you feel safe and comfortable getting back behind the wheel just because you feel like it, not because somebody expects you to. And in the short term, I want you to have a week away somewhere with sandy beaches and fruity drinks with little umbrellas."

She arched a brow at the shift from serious. "I'm in need of a tropical beach vacation?"

"Well, that one might be a little more for me since I'd be with you in that particular scenario. Swimsuits optional."

A week in an island cabana to explore every inch of that battle-hardened body? Yeah, she could get behind that. "I like the way you think."

"I've been giving that a lot of thought. But that's not the week we've got."

"No, it's not," she murmured. His week was supposed to be about Percy. She had more houses and businesses to decorate. And he'd be leaving soon.

It's not fair.

But life wasn't fair. She'd had that lesson driven home in ways that had scarred her body, and she'd had to work not to let it scar her mind. That had made her a woman who lived in the now, who savored the moment, and yet, with him, she found herself yearning for the what if, and with the yearning, aching. She turned to add the rest of the ingredients to the pot, mixing everything together as she struggled to breathe past the tightness in her chest.

"Look, Hannah, I want you. I think that's obvious. But I get that's a big thing and maybe more than you're willing to give under the circumstances. And that's absolutely fine. I get it. I won't be offended, and I won't push. Either way, you've given me enough fantasy fodder to fuel me for a good, long while."

"Fantasy fodder, huh?" She liked the idea of

him carrying a piece of her back with him, of being his fantasy. She desperately wanted this to be a beginning for them. She couldn't count on that, but her default position was one of optimism and hope, so she'd embrace it. Embrace him.

Giving the pot another stir, she put on the lid and turned down the heat. She turned back to him, settling her hands on his chest, needing to touch him, needing to feel the increasing thud of his heart under her palm. "You asked me what I want for myself. Right now, that's you."

Her gaze flicked up to his, and their eyes locked as his hands settled on her hips, holding her in place. But he remained silent, waiting for her to finish as the moment ran long, as the current that had crackled between them all week buzzed along her skin, and her breath all but stalled. "Instead of making ourselves crazy with the wondering or worrying, let's just start with that and see where it goes."

WAS THERE anything sexier than a woman who knew what she wanted?

And Hannah wanted him.

Thank God.

Ryan drew her in slowly, sliding one arm around to stroke up her spine and into her hair as he laid his lips over hers in a slow, simmering kiss. Without hesitation, she melted into him on a sigh that fired his blood. Whatever uncertainty or worry she'd been wrestling with, she'd made peace with it. Still, he had to let her set the pace, had to retain enough control to pull back if she changed her mind.

He tugged her more firmly against him, drinking in her ready, enthusiastic response and calculating routes to more comfortable horizontal surfaces. The bed was too far. Sofa was closer, and Percy wasn't due back for at least another hour.

Dragging his mouth from hers, he trailed kisses along her jaw, down her throat as she tipped her head back to give him access. Her little purr of pleasure had him going harder still, as her hands fisted in his shirt.

"Duke, stay." Ryan didn't wait to see if the dog followed his command before tugging Hannah toward the living room.

They tumbled onto the couch in a tangle of limbs and a fevered meeting of mouths. On the bottom, he shifted, gripping her legs and positioning her until she straddled him. The moment her center settled over his erection, she moaned low in her throat and rolled her hips. The breath backed up in his lungs and he started questioning his noble intentions of letting her take the lead.

Needing skin, he slid his hands beneath the hem of her sweater to skate up her back. So soft. He wanted to spend hours exploring the contours of her body, the contrast of her silken skin against his callused fingers. Hannah arched into his touch and broke the kiss to tug her sweater up and over her head, tossing it to the side.

His hands dug into her thighs as he took in the pretty red satin cupping her breasts like a gift. "Christ, you're beautiful."

Her nipples pearled against the fabric, and he reared up, taking one into his mouth.

"Oh, God." Arm locked around his head, she began to rock against him, mimicking the rhythm of his mouth.

Nuzzling, he managed to nudge the fabric aside until he closed his lips over her, swirling his tongue around the taut bud. Her whimper of pleasure had his cock jumping, and he arched against her. Her hands scrabbled at his shirt. With one hand, he reached back to yank it off, pitching it in the direction of the tree just as she slipped off her bra.

With a reverent curse, he kissed her again, cupping her breasts in both hands as she continued to rock against him. She was soft and warm and perfect in his palms, and the sounds she made as he rolled her nipples had his last shreds of control draining right out of his head. He needed her naked and mindless. Needed to bury himself inside her. But first he wanted her to fly apart for him.

His hand was at her zipper when Duke barked, the sound of it echoing from the foyer.

Hannah squeaked, jolting so hard, she fell right off him onto the floor.

"Shit, are you okay?"

"I'm—"

They both froze at the sound of the garage door.

"Percy!" Eyes going wide, Hannah scrambled for her bra.

Ryan tossed her the sweater and looked around for his shirt. He plucked it off the Christmas tree and yanked it on as the kitchen door opened. Hannah pulled on her sweater and hurled herself toward one end of the sofa, smoothing her hair as she went. Ryan flopped on the other end, adopting what he hoped was a relaxed posture just as Percy strolled in.

The old man had a spring in his step, and his gait was steadier than it had been when Ryan arrived last week. "Evenin', you two."

"You're home early." Ryan hoped that didn't sound like the accusation it was.

"We decided not to go to the show. Missed the beginning, and Betty's got an early start tomorrow."

"How was dinner?" Hannah's voice was too bright and cheery to be real.

A muscle twitched in Percy's jaw as his gaze slid back and forth between them. "It was good. We did a lot of talking about old times."

"Great. I'm gonna go check on the chili." She popped up like a jack-in-the-box and headed into the kitchen.

Percy watched her disappear. "Good night?"

"It's been fine. Why?"

"Your shirt's on inside out."

Well, hell.

Percy grinned. "Good for you, son." Calling to the dog, he raised his voice. "Duke and I are just gonna go upstairs and read a while. Y'all enjoy your chili."

Hannah didn't make a peep from the kitchen.

Ryan took the time to right his shirt before seeking her out. She was staring into the open fridge.

"Are we missing the sour cream?" he asked.

"I was contemplating whether I could crawl in here to die of mortification."

Ryan rubbed a hand over the back of his neck, as if that would dissipate the lingering sting of embarrassment, and moved to pull bowls from the cabinets and utensils from the drawer. "It's not that bad. And I officially owe Duke a bone or something for the heads-up."

"I'm bringing him a dozen of the peanut butter dog biscuits Carolanne carries at Sweet Magnolias."

"Seems fair. Dinner and a movie instead?"

"Sounds...well, not perfect, but very, very good."

He'd take the not perfect. And maybe it was for the best. His time with her had an expiration date, and they didn't have the luxury of spending all of it in bed. Maybe he needed to take this as a sign and establish a little distance. Slowly dial it back toward friends.

So their night home alone turned way more PG, as they finished the chili and curled up together to watch *Christmas In Connecticut*. Not at all his kind of movie, and not what he'd planned for the night, but he enjoyed himself anyway, loving the way she felt tucked up against him where he could play with the silk of her hair. The quiet was every bit as appealing as the heat. And wasn't that a surprise?

Once the movie was over, she rose and stretched. "I need to be getting home. I'm on early shift tomorrow."

Ryan drove her home. As they stopped under her porch light, he pulled her into his arms, lacing his hands at the small of her back. "Sorry Percy has continued his streak of shit timing."

Hannah's mouth quirked in a rueful smile. "Could've been worse. If we'd been upstairs, I doubt we'd have heard the dog."

The blood that had made its way back to his

brain promptly drained south again at the thought of what they could have been doing. "Better make that two dozen biscuits."

She was still laughing when he kissed her. The sweet, spicy taste of her seeped into him as her arms twined around his shoulders. He could do this every night. Surprised by the certainty of it, he pulled back.

Hannah smiled. "Thanks for a…memorable night."

"Back atcha. See you tomorrow?"

"Definitely. I get off at two." She hesitated. "Ryan?"

"Yeah?"

"You know how you wished for me to get to a place where I'm comfortable being behind the wheel, just because I feel like it?"

"Yeah."

"I don't know if I'm there yet, but would you drive with me tomorrow?"

This was a trust she'd offered no one else. It was another kind of intimacy—one that, in some ways, went deeper than the physical. Fear was a harder thing to share than pleasure. That she'd share hers with him, ask him to be there for this step, was humbling. Pride and something warmer slid through his chest, and he took a beat, accepted he was already past the point of pulling back, of returning to just friends.

He skimmed a thumb over her cheek, pleased when she tipped her face into his palm. "I'd be happy to."

She blew out a breath. "Okay."

"Okay."

"G'night." With one last brush of her lips, she opened the door.

Ryan waited until she'd gone inside, then strolled back to the truck. It was official. He was in over his head, way deeper than he'd intended. Right at the moment, he had a hard time caring. This was the most relaxed he'd been in years. All because of her. He was grateful she'd blown into his life, grateful she'd somehow scaled his defenses to show him she was the kind of woman he never knew he always wanted. What the hell that meant for them, he didn't know. But he suspected she'd be on the same page for finding out.

His phone rang as he slid into the driver's seat. Expecting his mom wanting an update on Percy, he fished it out. But it wasn't her number flashing on the screen.

"Hello?"

"Malone, it's Petrie."

At the deadly serious voice of Jerod Petrie, one of the members of his team, all Ryan's pleasure evaporated. Jerod was still in Afghanistan. He'd only be calling for one reason.

Tension coiled in his muscles. "What happened?"

In the silence, Jerod's sigh was heavier than an M1 Abrams tank. "I didn't want to call and tell you this on your time off, what with your family worries and all, but I knew you'd be more pissed if you didn't find out until you got back." He drew in a ragged breath. "Robbie Haskins is dead."

CHAPTER 9

"What's that frown for, sugar?" Mama Pearl nudged Hannah's shoulder. "Does somebody need some butt kickin' or some pie?"

Hannah's lips curved up at that. "There's always a reason for some of your pie."

Mama Pearl automatically lifted the dome off a beautiful lemon meringue and cut a piece. "Tell Mama Pearl what's wrong."

She loved this woman. "Nothing's wrong. At least, I don't think so. I just haven't heard back from Ryan today."

"Ah. The soldier. You been spendin' a lot of time with him the past couple weeks. Been smilin' more, too. And with you, that's saying somethin'."

Her cheeks heated and she forked up a bite of pie. "I like him." Okay, she'd edged well past the simple stage of *like*, but she didn't want to think about what that meant just yet. "Anyway, we're supposed to have plans this afternoon, but he hasn't answered my texts or phone call. That's not like him. I'm starting to worry something's happened to Percy."

"I reckon Percy's fine." Mama Pearl nodded toward the front window, where the man in question stood having a conversation with Duke.

The dog sat on the sidewalk, staring up at his new human with focus. Percy looped the leash around the bench by the front door and came inside. "Ladies."

"Hey, Percy. What brings you into town today?" Mama Pearl asked.

"Need a pie. I'm headed over to the senior

center for a poker tournament. Buy-in is dessert."

"You got a preference what kind?"

"Whatever I can get a whole one of."

"Coming' right up."

As Mama Pearl went to retrieve a fresh pie from the back, Hannah debated whether it made her nosy or needy to question Percy about Ryan. Ultimately, he took it out of her hands.

"You going by the house after you get off in a bit?"

"I'm not quite sure what I'm doing. Ryan's been incommunicado today."

"He woke up in a crap mood and got it into his head to tackle the garage. We've been working on it since first thing this morning. I doubt he's looked at his phone."

"Oh." Well, there was her explanation. Simple. "What's he in a bad mood about?"

"Don't rightly know. He didn't say and I didn't ask. But I figure you can cheer him right on up since that seems to be your super power."

"I expect I can make an effort in that direction."

"The poker tournament ought to last well into the evening, so you've got plenty of time."

Her face froze. Was he suggesting what she thought he was suggesting? She caught the twinkle in Percy's eyes. Mortified heat crawled up her throat and across her cheeks. "So you're saying we're on our own for dinner?"

"Sure. I used to be a helluva poker player, so I expect I'll be full up on sweets by then."

Translation: The house will be completely empty for hours.

Wondering if she could just sink through the floor and die of embarrassment, she choked out, "Noted."

Mama Pearl emerged with the pie, shooting a curious glance between the two of them before ringing Percy's order up.

"Good luck with the poker tournament."

"Thanks. I'm hoping somebody will be bringing baklava. My Janie used to make it for me. It's my favorite."

Carolanne made amazing baklava. Filing that detail away, Hannah waved and turned back to her pie. By the time she'd finished the pie and her shift, she'd worked her way through the embarrassment. Mostly. If Ryan's bad mood stemmed from sexual frustration, well, she could relate. She'd lain awake far too late last night, thinking about what they hadn't finished. So maybe it was worth putting off their plans of driving for far more pleasurable pursuits.

The garage door was down by the time Hannah made it to the house, so she trotted up the steps and knocked on the door. When Ryan didn't answer, she tried the knob. Locked. Maybe he was in the shower? Or working out back? Circling around the house, she scanned the backyard, but he wasn't out there. So she went back to the front door and rang the bell. This time the door was yanked open.

Her flirty smile slid away as she caught sight of Ryan's face. The stoic soldier mask was back, along with that unnatural stillness that had to be part of his training. "Hey. I tried to get up with you earlier."

"Sorry. I was busy."

"Percy came by the diner and said you'd been tackling the garage. That's quite the project." She stepped into the house and tried to slip her arms around him, but he stepped back.

The rejection struck her like a slap. He was hard-core walls up. Clearly, they weren't going to be picking up where they'd been interrupted last night. Not yet, anyway. Shoving down her disappointment and hurt, she slid her hands into her coat pockets. "What's wrong?"

"Nothing."

"Did you and Percy have a fight?"

"No." He grabbed his coat and the keys. "Let's get this over with."

Her pleasure at seeing him began to wane as he yanked the door open and gestured her ahead of him. In its place, the vague anxiety she always had when faced with the prospect of driving mushroomed up and pressed down on her like a cloud of ash. With every step out of the house, every foot closer to the truck, the pressure cranked tighter. At her back, she could feel his impatience, and her hands began to shake.

Clenching them into fists, she stopped before circling around to the driver's side. "You know what? Today's not a good day for this."

"It's fine. Just get in the truck."

The clipped tone had her hunching into her coat. No way was she getting behind the wheel with him in this kind of mood. "Ryan, I can't deal with your stress and mine. Something is clearly going on with you that you don't want to talk about. And that's fine. It's just not a good time. We'll do this later."

"Later," he snorted. "Sure. Just keep running away from your commitments because it's easier. Maybe you should just keep on walking."

Stunned, she could only stare at him. "Excuse me?"

"You're a coward. Hiding out from your life, making do with this small existence instead of taking the hard road and doing whatever's necessary to get back to your real life."

His words hit her like a hail of bullets, hard enough she stumbled back. What could she say? It was true. Her sister had been carefully tiptoeing around it for the past two months. But there was no reason for this implacable, hateful attitude. No reason that was about her, anyway. Because this wasn't the man she'd come to know.

"What happened after you left me last night?"

"Nothing."

"Something happened. Something tripped this switch, because the guy I've gotten to know over the past couple of weeks isn't an asshole."

"You wouldn't know what I am."

"I know you're hurting over something and lashing out." Nothing else made sense.

"You don't know anything. Newsflash, Elf Girl, the world isn't the happy, fluffy place you pretend it to be."

"I'm not pretending anything."

He snorted in disgust. "This was a mistake. All of this was a mistake." There was no question that by this he meant them.

She flinched back as if he'd slapped her, her back coming up against the truck. "You don't mean that."

"I mean every word."

Maybe he was right. Maybe she'd misjudged him from the beginning. Either way, she wasn't sticking around for more abuse. "Fine. I'm gonna go. If you decide to pull your head out of your ass, you know where to find me."

Her eyes burned with unshed tears as she strode down the driveway, everything he'd said banging around in her brain like so many bumper cars. As she reached the sidewalk, she turned back, taking in his stiff posture, his fisted hands, and the immutable set of his chin. "You know, maybe I am living small and in the grand scheme of things my life is insignificant, but it's better than this shadow of a life you insist on. At least I'm not afraid to let people love me."

His expression didn't even flicker.

Accepting the disappointment of that, she walked away.

RYAN NEEDED to get the hell out of Wishful. Everywhere he looked reminded him of Hannah and of the fact that he'd been here, enjoying life, instead of in Afghanistan, a part of the mission that had stolen his friend's life. The details Jerod had relayed about the op kept playing on repeat in his head. If he'd been there, he could've done something to stabilize Robbie long enough to make it to a fucking hospital. Instead, he'd died of the trauma before he'd even made it on the helo.

But he couldn't just leave. Not without completing the mission he'd been assigned here. Tired of waiting, of diplomacy, of pussyfooting around the realities, Ryan carried his medical bag downstairs. Percy sat at the kitchen table, digging into the spoils of his poker tournament win. Of course a grown-ass man should have pie at ten in the damned morning.

"Well, I see your mood hasn't improved. Have some pie, since you clearly didn't get anything *else* sweet this week."

No, he certainly hadn't. He'd poured gasoline all over his relationship with Hannah and set it on fire. "I don't want any damned pie. We're doing this exam. I need to get back to base, and I need to know you're okay before I go."

"You're not my doctor, and I don't need a damned exam to tell me what I already know. I'm old as dirt. End of story."

Ryan pinched the bridge of his nose. "Percy—"

"You think I don't know your mama sent you, no matter what bull you fed me when you got here? I'm no idiot. I let you stay because she's worried about you, too."

Ryan dropped his hand and stared at his uncle. Had his mother set him up this whole time? Surely she hadn't deliberately exaggerated Percy's condition to get him home from the field for this. Surely this was just something she'd said to Percy to cover up for what she'd really asked. Because the alternative didn't bear contemplating. "There's no reason to worry about me."

"Beg to differ, son. I was all set to send her back a report that everything was fine with you. But it's sure as shit not. Not after the last couple of days."

"I'm fine," Ryan gritted out. He wasn't going to let this get turned around on him.

"Bullshit. I'm not buying what you're selling. Not when you've been practically joined at the hip with Hannah since she first came over here, and she's been scarce as hen's teeth the last two days. Not when I got reports back that you made that sweet girl cry. Broke down right in the middle of decorating Maudie Bell's living room."

Fuck.

It wasn't a surprise. He'd been a right asshole. Deliberately striking out in a fashion that would ensure she wouldn't come anywhere near him again. Every word he'd spewed had made him feel lower than the belly of a worm. It had been like kicking a puppy. He'd told himself it was necessary. He didn't deserve someone like her in his life. Better he hurt her now, before it went any further. Before his darkness ended up tainting all that goodness and light.

But he'd made her cry. Damn it.

"What the hell is the matter with you?" Percy demanded.

Fighting the urge to hunch his shoulders, Ryan kept his voice low and even. "I told you from the beginning, I don't need a woman."

"And I told you you were full of shit. She was good for you. You were *happier* with her."

He didn't want to hear this. He didn't need the reminder of what he'd had that Robbie would never get a chance at. "What do you know, old man?"

"I know not to throw away the love of a good woman. It's the best damned thing that can happen to a man, and you're a damned moron if you think otherwise."

"Hannah doesn't love me." He'd torched things before they could get to that point. To save them both.

"She could've, if you'd kept your head out of your ass. But you had to go self-destructing shit. Because that's what you do."

Ryan's head kicked back. "What the hell are you talking about?"

"Ever since you went Delta Force, you've pulled back from everybody and everything. You deny yourself anything real or good. Like you don't have a right to that, given what you do."

Searching for calm, Ryan curled his hands around the back of a chair and tried to stay reasonable. This was basic shit that Percy ought to remember from his own stint in the military. "I can't afford to get attached."

"You're afraid to get attached."

Insult bloomed, along with a flicker of what could have been recognition. Hannah had made the same accusation. Ryan clenched his teeth against it until his jaw all but cracked. "I'm not afraid." He gritted the words with a deliberateness that bordered on menace.

"Then why the hell did you blow up one of the best things to ever happen to you?"

"Because she deserves better!" Ryan roared. Before the sound even faded, Duke had wedged himself under Percy's chair, making Ryan feel like even more of a dick.

Dropping a hand to stroke the dog, Percy kept his own voice soft. "You're damned right she does. She deserves an apology and groveling for your behavior. And an explanation for whatever set you off."

Ryan closed his eyes, seeing Hannah's face, pinched with hurt even as she reached out to him. *Something happened. Something tripped this switch, because the guy I've gotten to know over the past couple of weeks isn't an asshole.*

Even in the midst of taking the hits he was dishing out, she still tried to make a connection. Jesus. And he'd wanted it. He'd wanted it more than his next breath. He'd wanted to take her into his arms and let it all spill out. But he couldn't do that. He needed to lock his shit down and keep it that way.

A fresh flare of anger crawled through him on the heels of the pain. He wouldn't be in this position if not for her. He'd been absolutely fine compartmentalizing everything. He could function that way. Excel that way. And she came into his life, with her tinsel and ribbon and good cheer and big heart and just blew his walls all to hell. How was he supposed to go back to war, back to the job, without his armor?

Pissed off at her, at Percy, at the world in general, Ryan scooped up the keys to Smitty's piece of shit truck. "I'm going for a drive."

Somewhere in this town, there had to be a place he could blow off some steam.

CHAPTER 10

Hannah debated with herself the whole walk to Percy's house. Ryan hadn't tried to contact her in two days. Maybe it had been unrealistic to expect an apology. But she simply couldn't reconcile the hateful things he'd said to her with the guy she'd come to know. Somewhere, deep down, he'd been doing it on purpose to push her away. She was a convenient target for some other hurt. Or maybe those were more attempts at justification for his behavior. None of it made the situation hurt any less.

She'd ended up breaking down at Maudie Bell Ramsey's house. Poor Chester had patted her back and offered up a plate of brownies, probably in the hopes that eating and sobbing weren't compatible. The older woman had tried to get her to talk about it, but Hannah hadn't wanted to admit how foolish she'd been in allowing herself to get attached to Ryan in the first place. Oh, who was she kidding? She'd fallen in love with the guy she'd believed him to be. And he hadn't wanted that. He'd been clear from the beginning what this was, what it could be. She'd just believed he'd been changing his mind and coming around to her way of thinking. Her mistake.

So instead of spilling her guts to one of the Casserole Patrol—who she suspected would've told her compatriots and headed over to Percy's en masse to "jerk a knot in Ryan's tail" as Maudie Bell had said—Hannah had finished the decorating job and gone home to Carolanne. The whole story had spilled out, along with gallons of tears. And because her sister was awesome, they'd turned to baking therapy and made baklava from scratch. Hannah had packed up a tin full of it to bring to Percy as a Christmas present. She wanted him to have another sweet reminder of his Janie.

She could just drop it off, all casual-like. *Don't mind me, I'm just armed with sugar and Christmas cheer.* But as she neared the house, her feet hesitated. What if Ryan was there? A part of her was afraid she'd see him. What if their next encounter proved he was actually the mean, hateful asshat and she'd been wrong about him all along? She didn't want confirmation that her judgment was so skewed. But another bigger part of her worried she wouldn't see him. That he'd maybe already gone—either home or back to Afghanistan—without an apology or a goodbye. The idea of it made her heart crack just a little bit more. She'd gotten her acceptance letter from the small business incubator and her first instinct had been to share the news with him. Would he even care?

She straightened her shoulders. It didn't

matter. She wasn't going to the house for Ryan. She was going for Percy. No matter how little she apparently meant to his nephew, she'd grown fond of the old man. She wasn't going to balk at giving him this gift out of some kind of cowardice. Moving briskly, she rounded the corner onto Cochran Drive. The house came into view...with no rattle-trap truck in the drive. Relief came first, draining some of the tension from her shoulders. On its heels came disappointment. She wanted...well, she didn't know what she wanted other than the guy she'd gotten to know. But that guy could never have spoken to her the way he had.

Moving quickly up the walk, Hannah's gaze skimmed over the greenery, the lights, and ribbons. All the hard work she and Ryan had done to bring some joy back to Percy. It was still beautiful, even in the daylight. She'd see Percy again when she came to take it all down. By then, Ryan would certainly be gone, if he wasn't already, and maybe Percy would have some kind of answers for her. Or maybe they'd pretend nothing had ever happened.

She rang the bell. Inside, Duke began to bark. Fidgeting on the front porch, she waited. But there was no shushing of the dog and no one answered the door. Maybe Ryan and Percy had gone off somewhere together. Although, Percy had been taking Duke almost everywhere. Inside, the dog's barking got more insistent. Uneasy, she tried the knob. Locked, of course. Just in case, she decided to circle around to the back, to peek inside.

Cupping a hand around her eyes, she peered through the window of the back door. Duke leapt up, booming bark startling her so badly she jerked back. Pressing a hand to her thundering heart, she bent forward again, scanning the kitchen. A corduroy clad leg and a bedroom slipper stuck out past the kitchen table.

"Percy!" She jiggled the knob. Also locked. She began to pound on the door. "Percy!"

The leg didn't move. Inside, Duke paced, interrupting his barking to whine.

Dropping the tin, she raced back around to the front of the house, lifting and shifting every pot, every plant, every piece of furniture or decoration she could think of that might hide a key. Rising to her toes, she ran her hands up and over the top of the door frame. No key. She scanned the flower beds, searching for a rock that wasn't really a rock. But there was nothing at all like that amid the mulch and bushes. Maybe she could get the garage door to lift. Rushing to the side of the house, she tried to get a grip on the door, but couldn't manage to budge it. She needed something to wedge beneath the lip to get some leverage. But there was nothing. Ryan had cleaned up the mess all around the house while he'd been here.

Duke's barking rose in pitch.

She had to get inside that house. Determined, she ran back up to the front door and rammed her shoulder into it. Pain ricocheted down her shoulder as she bounced off. That clearly wasn't going to work. Frantic, she whipped out her phone to dial 911, just as the truck rumbled into the drive with Ryan at the wheel.

THE LONG DRIVE around Hope Springs had done little to improve Ryan's mood. All he'd managed was an hour and a half of self-recriminations, backed up with a repeated chorus in Percy's voice, reminding him that he owed Hannah an apology. He'd do it before he left town, for whatever good it would accomplish. Maybe it would give her closure. For him, it would simply be another sign of how he'd fucked up.

Movement caught his eye as he pulled into the drive next to Percy's SUV. Hannah flew down the porch steps, toward the truck. The potent mix of joy and shame at the sight of her was a punch to the gut. He hadn't driven her away completely. But as he slid out of the driver's seat, he got a good look at her ashen cheeks and the eyes peeled wide with fear.

"Percy! Percy's passed out in the kitchen. I can't get in!"

For one, chilling beat, Ryan allowed the terror. Then he locked it away, throwing himself into action. He flew past her, hitting the porch steps at a dead run. His hand fumbled the key as he jammed it into the lock, and he lost precious seconds getting it to turn instead of simply kicking the door down as he'd done his first night here. Inside, Duke was going nuts.

Hannah's footsteps sounded behind him as he got the door open. They raced inside, following the frantic barking of the dog into the kitchen. Percy lay face down on the tile floor. One of the chairs was askew, as if he'd grabbed for it on the way down. A quick, visual assessment didn't indicate any obvious broken bones.

Behind him, Hannah gasped. "Oh my God!"

"Dial 911." He knelt, checking for a pulse. The beat of it pounded beneath his fingers. Dimly, he was aware of Hannah giving her name and the address as he gently rolled Percy over.

Percy moaned. "Janie? Is that you, baby?"

"Percy, it's Ryan. Can you hear me?"

The old man moaned. Ryan checked his head for injury, but found no evidence of trauma. Why the hell had he passed out? Snapping his head up, he scanned the counter, noted the usual, huge collection of empty glasses. The three-quarters eaten pie was still on the kitchen table. Suspicion dawning, Ryan bent low to check his breath, catching the telltale fruity scent.

"Tell them we have an eighty-one-year-old male in probable diabetic ketoacidosis. Rapid heartbeat, incoherent and only semi-responsive."

As she relayed the information, Ryan leapt to his feet and filled one of the glasses with water. Back down on the floor, he scooped an arm behind Percy's frail shoulders and lifted him. "Come on, Percy. You gotta get some water." As he pressed the glass to Percy's lips, he flailed, knocking the glass away and spilling the contents down his front.

"Damn it, Percy."

The tap switched on and a moment later, Hannah handed over another glass. Ryan tried again, taking a firmer grip on the old man's arms. Percy tossed his head from side to side, but Ryan held firm, managing to get a little water in him.

"What's the ETA of the ambulance?" he demanded.

"They don't know. There was a massive, multi-car pile up at the edge of town because of the Christmas parade. There's no ambulance available."

Fuck.

"She says they can send somebody from the Volunteer Fire Department until an ambulance is free."

"No time. He might slip into a coma before then. We've got to get him to the hospital now."

She relayed their intent to the dispatcher.

Percy's head lolled back. Ryan shook him. "Percy. Percy! Wake the hell up. You can't go to sleep. Stay with me now."

He groaned, his eyes fluttering.

"Tell me what to do." Hannah's voice shook.

"Find Percy's keys. They're probably on the hook by the front door."

She sprinted out of the room, back only a few seconds later with the keys in her hands. "Now what?"

"Grab a few of the water bottles in the fridge."

He shifted, scooping Percy into his arms. His weight was so slight as to be insubstantial, as if he were fading away already. Ryan should've figured it out sooner. He should've seen. He should've forced Percy to a doctor. Shoving away the guilt and thread of panic, he moved to the front door.

Hannah pulled it open, staying back a moment to nudge the dog back inside. Duke howled a protest at being left behind, but there was no place for him at the hospital. As soon as the door was shut, she skirted around him, yanking open the door to the backseat of Percy's SUV. Ryan settled him inside, buckling him in to keep him from slumping over, and crawled in with him.

"Give me the water."

She passed it over and he twisted off the cap, automatically pressing the bottle to Percy's lips and tipping it back. At least half dribbled over his chin, but some of it went in. The old man's throat worked as he swallowed.

"Good. That's good, Percy. Keep drinking."

"What—"

His gaze snapped to Hannah's. "I have to stay back here with him to monitor his vitals and try to keep him awake while I force some water down him. You've got to drive."

If possible, her face went paler. But she didn't argue, hesitating only a moment before rounding the vehicle to get into the driver's seat. She slid behind the wheel, her breathing way too fast. It wooshed in and out, a ragged, sawing sound. From the back seat, Ryan spared her a glance. She shook like a leaf. In the rearview mirror, he spotted the tears streaming down her cheeks and the edge of full-blown panic written all over her face.

Shit.

Percy's life depended on him getting this right. Modulating his voice to soothe, he said, "Breathe, Hannah. Slow it down. In for four, out for eight."

Hands white-knuckled on the wheel, she did as he asked.

"You're going to put the key in the ignition and crank the vehicle. Keep breathing."

With a jerky nod, she followed orders.

"Check your mirrors, then put the car in reverse. We're going to head to the hospital, and you're going to do fine. It's a short drive, and I'm right here with you."

Another jerky nod, a few more breaths that had him wanting to scream, then she started the car and backed into the street. He could only pray they'd be fast enough.

CHAPTER 11

*H*annah blinked furiously against the
tears that wouldn't seem to stop.
Every muscle in her body ached with tension as
she gripped the steering wheel, like that was
going to offer her some kind of control of the
situation. With every foot of travel, she waited
for the flashback or the uncontrollable shaking.

From the backseat, Ryan's harsh voice
snapped, "Come on, old man. Don't you dare
make me call Mom. You know she'll be down
here in a minute to nurse you and drive you

batshit. You want to avoid that, you stay awake!"

The whip of it made her flinch, even though it wasn't directed at her.

As if he'd noticed her reaction, he spoke again. "You're doing great. If you haven't already, hit the emergency flashers."

She hadn't even thought of that. With trembling fingers, she stabbed the button.

"There now. That's good. Drink some more water."

The water bottle crackled, followed by a retching sound.

"Shit. That's okay. That's fine. We'll clean it up later. Try to get some more down."

"Do…do I need to speed up?"

"If you can."

Hannah sucked in a breath. The faster she went, the faster this would be over. She pressed the accelerator.

It was the longest four miles of her life.

By the time they lurched to a stop outside

the Emergency Department of Wilton Memorial Hospital, her stomach threatened to revolt.

"Run in, get a nurse," Ryan ordered.

More than ready to get out of the driver's seat, she hurled herself out of the SUV, nearly falling as her legs trembled with relief that they'd made it. That help was just on the other side of those doors. She stumbled into the ER. "Help, please. We've got an eighty-one year old man in the car in—" What had Ryan said? "—probable diabetic ketoacidosis. He's barely conscious."

The nurse manning the desk made a call and suddenly everybody was in motion. A gurney appeared from somewhere and a group of people rushed outside. Shaking with the chill of lingering panic, Hannah trailed after them, giving the whole crew a wide berth as they transferred Percy out of the backseat. Over the roar in her ears, she could just hear Ryan spouting off medical stuff she didn't really understand. Percy's skin was flushed and his chest heaved with big, gasping breaths, as if his lungs weren't working right.

As the automatic doors slid open, someone asked Ryan, "Are you family?"

He hesitated. "It's complicated."

She didn't hear the response. Someone else had pulled up behind the SUV. She had to move it out of the way. On another deep breath, she made herself get back in, taking another couple of deep breaths in hopes of calming her nerves before she shifted into drive. It took mere minutes to park and run back up to the building. No incidents either time. She didn't have the bandwidth to think about that as she raced back inside.

Ryan stood in front of the double doors leading to the treatment rooms, his hands loose, shoulders slumped. The raw, unguarded fear in his face simply gutted her. In that moment, it didn't matter that he'd been an asshole. It didn't matter what he'd said. He looked like a man washed up on a foreign shore, and she couldn't just leave him there alone.

Without a word, she wrapped her arms around his waist, willing him to take the comfort she offered. On a pained sound, he curled around her, burying his face in her hair and holding on tight. She fisted her hands in his jacket, a fresh knot of tears clogging her throat as she breathed in the scent of him. And for just a moment, it didn't matter how she'd gotten here. She was back in his arms, and the warmth of him thawed the last, lingering cold of fear from facing her demons and the sickness at how they'd parted.

They stood that way for a long time, until the next incoming emergency forced them to relocate out of the path of foot traffic. But he didn't let her go.

Gripping tight to her hands he stared down into her face. "You drove."

"I guess I did."

"You were amazing."

She shook her head. "It wasn't—"

"Don't say it wasn't a big deal. I know it was for you. And I'm grateful you pushed through your fear for Percy. If we hadn't gotten him here this fast…"

"He's going to be okay." She knew no such thing, but her default state was optimism, and whether it was true or not, they both needed the lie.

"I know my opinion shouldn't matter, and I know you probably don't ever want to see me again, but I'm proud of you."

"I…Thank you." His opinion did matter. A part of her wanted to flush with pleasure at his praise, but talking about all this with Percy's life hanging in the balance left her uneasy.

Dipping his head, he seemed to search for words. The discomfort in his eyes was palpable. "I want to say, too, that I'm sorry. I was a jerk. I don't have any excuse. But I'd like to tell you the reason, if you'll listen. I feel like I owe you that."

She wanted that reason. Had driven herself crazy the last couple of days trying to imagine what it might be so that his behavior made some kind of sense. But she didn't need it right this second. "It can wait until we get through all this. You'll have paperwork and whatever else. And people to call about Percy's status, right?"

"Yeah, I guess so." He reached up to rub the back of his neck. "Under the circumstances, I don't have any right to ask you this but..."

Calling herself ten kinds of fool, she stepped into him. "Of course, I'll stay."

Some of the tension seemed to leech out of his frame and he dropped his brow to hers. "Thank you."

"Mr. Malone?"

Hannah recognized the brunette nurse as Corinne McGee, one of the diner's former waitresses. She had a clipboard in her hand.

"We've got Mr. Gannaway on fluids and are monitoring his condition closely. He's not out of the woods yet, but you were spot-on in your diagnosis."

Ryan's expression shifted back into professional mode, but his fingers tightened around hers. "Is there a prognosis yet?"

"The doctor will be out to talk with you as soon as she can."

He simply nodded. To anyone who didn't know him, he'd appear calm and collected, totally in control. But his brittle edges stood out to her like flares. If anything happened to Percy…

No. Nothing was going to happen to Percy. He was going to be fine. They'd gotten him here in time, and she refused to acknowledge any other outcome. One of them had to maintain some optimism. Ryan was far too close to breaking.

Corinne held out the clipboard. "I understand you aren't exactly family, but as you were the one who brought him in, can you fill out as much of this paperwork as you can?"

"Of course."

As soon as they sat down, he stared at the forms as if they were in a whole other language. Hannah's heart pinched at seeing him anything other than a hundred percent capable. He was so used to taking care of everybody else, she didn't think he ever acknowledged he needed someone to take care of him. She wanted to do that for him, wanted to ease this burden.

She squeezed his arm. "Maybe I should get us some coffee."

"Yeah, okay."

She rose just as the exterior doors slid open again and someone walked in with a service dog. The sight of it snapped her brain into gear again. "Oh my God, Duke!"

"What?"

"He's probably going nuts in the house. We just left him." Was this what had happened with his previous owner?

"I didn't even think about him." Ryan rubbed at his temple, as if this was one more thing he wasn't sure he could handle.

This, at least, she could fix. "It'll be fine. I'll get him taken care of."

He shot her a look of gratitude as she pulled out her phone and dialed. "Brooke. It's Hannah. I need a favor."

∾

OVER THE LONG HOURS, the ER waiting room had mostly emptied out. Ryan had done his duty, calling all the family who was still waiting for word. His mom had been ready to drive down on the spot, but he'd urged her to wait until there was more definitive news on Percy's condition. Hannah had made arrangements for Brooke to keep Duke until they were free to come get him, so that was one less detail to worry about. She'd also called Betty and the rest of the Casserole Patrol, who'd set up a vigil for several hours in one corner of the waiting room. He'd finally convinced them to go home around midnight, with promises he'd send word if anything changed before morning.

Hannah yawned, her head dropping to his shoulder. For a long moment, he enjoyed the comfort of the weight of her against him. A solid, steady presence. He couldn't have gotten through this without her. Not in his current mental state over things with his team, with Robbie. But it wasn't fair to take advantage of her and expect her to stick it out the rest of the night.

"You don't have to stay."

She didn't even lift her head. "Yes I do. I've already taken off tomorrow. I'm not leaving you here alone."

He didn't deserve her kindness.

"Everyone deserves kindness," she murmured.

Apparently, he'd spoken aloud. "I didn't treat you with kindness." It was the truth and it was out there. He might as well make his apologies and address it, even if it pushed her away. "I'm sorry I behaved like a jackass."

She straightened. "You said you had a reason."

That reason detonated in his head, his heart, as his brain conjured images of his friend. Of the smile and the terrible jokes he'd never hear again.

Ryan took a slow breath. "This is the longest stretch I've been off in about four years. I've been on deployment, going from mission to mission with my team. When you're out there, in the middle of all the violence, it gets where that's the only thing you can see. It's the only thing you know. I didn't think too much about it. Part of our training involves compartmentalization. We deal with what's in front of us. Nothing more, nothing less. And we don't get attached to much outside the team. It's normal. Our normal, anyway. I don't know when I stopped expecting more, stopped seeing anything else."

His thumb stroked along the back of her hand, taking comfort, even now. Her face held no judgment, just patience and curiosity.

"But you made me think about it. You made me want something else. Sometime while I've been here, you blew that objectivity and compartmentalization all to hell. I stayed longer than I intended, partly because of Percy's lack of cooperation, but partly because I didn't want to go back. I didn't want to walk away from you. I started thinking about all those what ifs I don't allow myself in the field. About what it would be like to not be dealing with battle trauma and death. To get out, go to med school, and specialize in something where seeing my patients doesn't remind me of my failures. Where nobody's permanently maimed or dying. And I want that so fucking bad, I can taste it."

The hand he held tightened around his fingers. "There's no shame in that."

He dropped his head. She had no idea how much shame there was in that for him. "Right after I left you the other night, I got a call from a friend. One of our team was injured on an op. There was a fucking trip wire and a homemade bomb. Robbie didn't survive long enough to make it on the helo for extraction and treatment."

"Jesus. I'm so sorry." She pressed a cheek against his shoulder, just holding on, and he welcomed it even as he cursed himself for the weakness of needing it. Needing her.

"I should've been there. If I'd been there, I could've done something. And instead I was here, with you, pretending I could have another life."

For a long moment, she stayed silent. "Am I correct in assuming that they wouldn't have run the mission without another medic as part of the team?"

"Yeah."

"Another medic with the same training as you?"

"Yes, but—"

"No, no buts. You cannot blame yourself for this, Ryan. The only one at fault here is who-ever set up that tripwire. Not you, not whoever was standing in your stead, not anyone else on your team. Be angry. Grieve the loss. But don't blame yourself."

There were sense and logic to her words, and everything in him wanted to reject them. "Easier said than done."

"If you'd pulled away from me sooner, if you'd been there for Robbie, you wouldn't have been here today for Percy. Even if I'd managed to get in the door, I wouldn't have known what was wrong or what to do. I'd have waited for the fire department, if for no other reason than I wouldn't have been physically able to get Percy off the floor. I wouldn't have had the training to know he needed water or that he needed to stay awake."

It was easy, far too easy, to see the picture she painted. To see the probable outcome. He wanted to block it out, deny the possibility, but she was still talking.

"There was a medic on the team, and Robbie didn't make it. Maybe if you'd been the medic, Robbie still wouldn't have made it, and that's horrible and tragic. But then Percy might be gone, too. And that wouldn't have been your fault either, because even here, outside a war-zone, tragedies just happen. There's only one of you, and you can't carry everyone on your shoulders, no matter how impressive they are. No matter how much you believe you can con-trol everything, you can't. And I think, some-where deep down, you know that."

Knowing and accepting were two very different things.

"The other day, you accused me of hiding out from my life, of making do with what I have here instead of doing whatever was necessary to get back to my real life."

Hearing his words, Ryan winced. "I can't believe I said that to you. I was wrong. Dead wrong."

"I accept your apology. But you weren't speaking to me, were you? Not really. You were angry with yourself because you don't want to go back."

"Yes," he whispered.

"Then maybe you shouldn't."

He whipped his head toward her. "What?"

"If you've reached a point where you're that reluctant and conflicted about going back after a few weeks off, if you're questioning your ability to compartmentalize yourself in order to do the job, then maybe you're getting to the point where you shouldn't be doing the job."

That there was more than a kernel of truth

to what she said scared him down to the marrow. He wanted the choice. All those down-the-road plans were for when he was ready to walk away. He didn't want to be forced into the decision because he wasn't capable anymore. He wanted to leave on a high note. On his own terms. Not as a failure. "It's not that easy. I have obligations to my team, a contract. I—"

She held up a hand. "I'm not saying walk away today. But give yourself permission to think about it. Seriously consider it. You chose an incredibly difficult profession. I can't even fathom how hard you worked to get where you are. One of the elite. But you can only do that effectively if you can maintain your edge. Psychologically, that's got to wear on a person. That doesn't make you weak or a failure. It makes you human."

Somehow, staring into her big, blue eyes, that didn't seem like such a bad thing. How was it that this woman understood him so well after so little time? How had he come to crave that so much, so fast?

"Mr. Malone?"

He jolted at the voice, rising to his feet as the doctor approached him. A white lab coat flapped around her legs.

"I'm Dr. Campbell. I wanted to let you know that Mr. Gannaway is going to be okay. We've stabilized him, and expect him to make a full recovery, though we'd like to keep him for a full forty-eight hours to make sure we get his levels worked out. Provided everything goes as expected, he can go home Christmas Day."

"That's fantastic news. Thank you."

"However—"

Of course there was a "but" to this scenario.

"He's got to start taking care of himself. I'll be making recommendations for follow-up care so he can learn how to manage his diabetes," she said.

Thinking of the mission that brought him to Wishful, he scooped a hand through his hair. "Let's get down to brass tacks, Doc. Does he need assisted living?"

"That depends on how well Percy will take care of himself."

Hannah spoke up. "If Percy gets the proper nutrition and exercise, is there any reason he shouldn't be able to stay in his own home?"

"I don't see why not. His mind is just fine."

Ryan exhaled. That wouldn't stop his mom from worrying, but it would certainly go a long way toward making Percy happy.

"You two should go get some rest. He's sleeping comfortably now. Come on back by in the morning and you'll be able to talk with him. He'll be a lot more coherent then."

He shook Dr. Campbell's hand. "Thank you."

"Thank you. Your diagnosis and quick thinking saved his life."

The knots he'd been carrying around for hours finally eased the rest of the way.

"I understand you're an Army medic? Special forces?" she said.

He frowned. "How did you—"

Dr. Campbell smiled. "Percy's quite the talker. Anyway, if you ever decide to hit up med school when you get out, you've got the makings of a solid physician."

"Thanks."

As the doctor headed back through the double doors, he stretched his aching back. "I'll take you home."

Hannah shook her head. "I don't want to get home this late. My sister will be waking up in a couple of hours for the bakery, and I don't want to inadvertently wake her up early." She slipped her hand into his and tipped those baby blues up to his. "I'd rather stay with you."

A curious mix of gratitude and awareness slid through him. This woman would never cease to surprise him. Tightening his hand around hers, he tugged her toward the door. "Let's go home."

CHAPTER 12

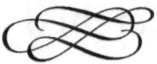

"I can't believe scratching the front door was the only damage Duke did." Hannah ran her fingers over the gouges from the dog's claws. "Poor baby must've thought he was being abandoned again."

"Can't blame him for that. I can fix it. But it can wait until tomorrow." Ryan jerked his head toward the stairs. "C'mon. I'll get you something to sleep in."

Exhaustion from the long day weighed her steps as she followed him. But along with the bone-deep tired, her heart was lighter for having cleared the air between them. She hadn't been wrong about him. Hadn't been wrong about the kind of man he was. Though, after tonight, she wondered if maybe he was wrong about himself. But those were thoughts that required more brainpower than she currently possessed.

The guest room he occupied was neat as a pin, hardly showing evidence he'd been living there. That was no surprise. She remembered how little he'd come with. The bag he'd carried that first day was tucked neatly into a corner, and she spied a neat line of toiletries arranged on the bathroom counter. Was he naturally this neat, or was that his military training?

Ryan opened a drawer and pulled out a t-shirt. "Is this okay? I don't have much here."

"I'm sure it's fine."

He didn't let go as she accepted the shirt. "Thank you for taking care of me today."

Her lips curved a little. "It's the people who take care of everybody else who sometimes need caretaking the most."

He was suddenly far too serious. "I didn't know I did."

Her heart pinched at the rare show of vulnerability. She kept her voice soft. "And now that you know?"

"I don't know." The admission was grudging, and she knew how much he had to hate the reality of it.

"Nothing wrong with that. Nobody said you have to have all the answers right now."

"Good thing. I feel like I don't have any of the answers. You've just made me ask a whole lot more questions."

"I consider that a success. I wanted to change your view of things. Though, I confess, that wasn't exactly the kind of rocking your world I intended." She slapped a hand over her mouth, barely trapping the giggle that wanted to spill out. "Sorry. I have no filter when it's late."

His eyes went dark, and his faint smile was sharp as a blade. "I definitely feel like I missed out on that particular variety."

She swallowed, a frisson of awareness racing down her spine, along her skin. The hunger in his gaze banished her exhaustion, banished any lingering doubts. Tossing the shirt aside, she stepped into him. "No reason to miss out. You're still here."

"For now."

"We only have the now." As a reminder to them both, she kissed him.

His hands dove into her hair, as he angled his mouth more firmly against hers, and she wrapped around him. His growing erection pressed against her belly. Opening to him, she gloried in the sweep of his tongue against hers. His fingers combed through her hair, stroking down her spine and over her ass, drawing her hips against his. She rose to her toes in an attempt to better line them up. Hooking his hands behind her thighs, he lifted her as if she weighed nothing, settling her exactly where she wanted to be. Tightening her legs around his hips, she pulled his hardness closer to her core.

He growled, turning them toward the bed,

lowering her to the mattress. It sank beneath their combined weight, squeaking faintly as they dove at each other, their hands busy tugging, touching, taking, stripping each other down between frenzied, frantic kisses. When his mouth closed over her breast, she cried out, arching up and digging her fingers into the muscles of his magnificent shoulders. Her hands fumbled with his belt as he continued to kiss and suckle. At last, she managed to defeat the button and zipper of his jeans, making enough space to slide her hand inside and wrap her fingers around him.

He cursed, his own fingers swift and efficient as he stripped her the rest of the way, leaving her bare. His gaze raked over her in frank appreciation.

"Damn, you're beautiful."

"So are you."

The bedside lamp painted the muscles of his arms and chest in shadow as he bent again to kiss and touch and stroke. His hand covered her sex, firm and possessive, and she arched up, needing more. More pressure, more friction. Just more.

"Ryan, please."

Parting her folds, he stroked a lazy finger around her clit and through the wet heat between her thighs before sliding one finger inside her. She cried out, bucking her hips as he continued to rub.

"More."

He slid in another finger, adding a twist of his wrist that had her flying apart in seconds. He wrung out every atom of pleasure, until she lay boneless and gasping. By the time she came fully back to herself, he wore a smirk of male satisfaction.

She found it hard to mind. "I'd forgotten what it was like to have a non-battery-assisted orgasm." She clapped her hands over her mouth again, cursing her lack of filter.

The smirk turned into a full on grin. "Better than you remembered?"

"Way better. Now come here and show me

the rest of the ways you're superior to my battery-powered buddy."

"Yes, ma'am."

Foil crackled and a few moments later, he crawled over her, settling into the cradle of her hips. Needing to touch him, she wrapped her hand around his length, stroking from base to tip and back before aligning him with her entrance. Bracing his arms on either side of her, he pressed slowly forward, sinking into her, stretching and filling, inch by slow inch. They both groaned as he found his way fully home.

"Hannah."

He lowered to kiss her, deep and gentle, and lacing his fingers with hers, began to move. She held his gaze as the pleasure built. With every stroke, the walls he'd put up between them were falling. And then they were both spinning out over the edge in a spectacular free fall.

At length their breathing slowed. Above her, he stirred. "You were right."

"About what?"

"Rocking my world."

She couldn't help it. The giggle burst free. "You rocked mine pretty thoroughly, too."

"I'd like to rock it again in the very near future, but I think we kinda have to sleep."

"There's always the morning. I mean, I don't know about you, but that seems like a really good start to the day."

He brushed a kiss over her lips. "I like the way you think."

Once they'd taken care of the necessities, they crawled back into bed together, his front to her back, and he curled around her. She didn't bother with the t-shirt, since he was a living furnace. It was pretty damned cozy and perfect. He fell into silence, and she wondered if he'd fallen asleep. She'd get there herself, in a little while. For just a few more minutes, she wanted to bask.

"Can I ask you something?"

She jerked herself back from the edge of dreams. "Sure."

His hand stroked idly over her hip. "I don't have any right to even bring this up because I know what I'm asking. But I'm going to ask anyway."

Rousing herself, she flipped over to face him. This sounded like a Serious Thing. "What?"

He exhaled slowly, resuming the stroking along her hip, a petting she'd come to recognize as a form of self-comfort. "How do you feel about long distance relationships?"

Her smile spread so wide, she wondered if he could see it in the dark. Just in case he couldn't, she leaned in to kiss him. "Extremely amenable."

"Really? Because my schedule is insane, and I won't always be able to say where I am or when I'll make it home again. I can't always talk on a regular schedule. I don't even know when I'll be able to next get leave and—"

She pressed a finger to his lips. "Stop trying to talk me out of it. The answer's still yes."

Curling a hand around hers, he pressed a kiss to her open palm. "Okay."

She snuggled in against him, safe and warm

and so full of joy and hope for the future she all but glowed with it. "Ryan? There's just one more thing."

"What?"

"Merry Christmas Eve."

RYAN TUCKED a firm hand under Percy's elbow as they got out of the SUV.

"For the love of God, I'm not an invalid," Percy groused.

"You literally just spent two days in the hospital. No arguing about taking a little help."

With a huff, he shuffled his slow way toward the front porch, muttering about being forced to use a wheelchair at the hospital and how long discharge had taken.

"Yeah, well, that would've gone quicker without your entourage, but there is no turning away the Casserole Patrol," Hannah told him.

"Truer words," Percy intoned.

"I think Miss Betty's got a crush on you," Ryan teased.

Color leapt in the old man's cheeks, a welcome reprieve from how he'd looked in the hospital lying against the harsh white sheets in the sterile room.

"It's true," Hannah put in, shouldering the bag with all the new diabetic testing supplies. "She helped stock your kitchen while you were laid up. Everything's set for you to transition to your new lifestyle. Her daughter's diabetic, so she knows all about it."

Percy cut a glance at Ryan. "Aren't you gonna be riding my ass about this new diagnosis? Telling me all the stuff I can't eat anymore, all the new crap I've got to do?"

"Nope. I figure you got enough of that at the hospital, and you'll get more in the future as you sort out how to manage it. But today is Christmas, and I'm just happy you're still around to celebrate it with us."

He ducked his head, but not before Ryan

caught the gleam of tears. "Wouldn't be if not for you two. Thank you."

Hannah scooted up to his other side, slipping her arm through his in a gesture that was as much affection as assistance. "We're just glad you're okay."

They reached the top of the steps without incident, and Ryan loosened his grip, satisfied that Percy was moving well enough on his own.

"You should both be with your own families, not fussing over an old cuss like me."

"I had Christmas with my sister this morning, and we did lunch before Ryan and I left to pick you up."

He grunted. "I still don't feel right about keeping you away from your mama, with you being stateside for the holiday. She gets to see you little enough."

"Yeah, about that," Ryan muttered.

The front door flew open and a chorus of "Merry Christmas, Percy!" about knocked them backward.

"What the—?" Percy's eyes went wide as

Ryan's parents and both his brothers spilled out, surrounding them.

"We brought Christmas to you," he murmured.

His mother, Trisha, wrapped Percy in a hug. "Oh, it's so good to see you, Uncle Percy."

"You're here." Percy's voice quavered. "You're all here on Christmas Day. Why?"

"You refused to come to us and we refused to take no for an answer, you stubborn old coot. We love you. Now come on inside. We've got a massive spread and dinner's just about to come out of the oven." Not allowing an argument, Trisha ushered him through the door.

At the panicked plea in Percy's eyes, Ryan lifted his hands in a what-can-I-do? gesture. His mom was taking over now. That was the end of that.

With probably more fanfare than Percy liked and a helluva lot of talking, they finally got him settled in the living room. Duke, released by one of Ryan's brothers from the crate they'd gotten yesterday, gave a joyful bark and whine, offering up a full-body wag and wriggle, pressing himself against Percy's legs.

"Hey. Hey there, buddy. I'm happy to see you, too." He bent low, rubbing and petting the dog, pressing his face into the brown and black fur. "I'm happy to see everybody."

Ryan met Hannah's gaze across the room, matching her brilliant smile with one of his own. Filling the house with family to greet Percy when he got home had been her idea, and the moment he'd called his mother to put in the request, Trisha had begun orchestrating the moving of the holiday with all the efficiency of a three-star general. It had absolutely been the right call.

At a few words from Trisha, everybody descended on the kitchen to finish food prep and begin setting the table. Left alone with Percy, Ryan propped a shoulder against the mantle and watched him with the dog.

Hands still buried in Duke's fur, Percy met his gaze. "Thank you for this. Thank you for everything you've done while you were here. I didn't want any help, didn't want to admit I needed it."

"Yeah, I get that. Pot, kettle, and all that. And you're welcome. It's been a good little vacation." With a pang of regret, he straightened. "In less awesome news, I have to head back to Fort Polk tonight to catch a MAC flight back overseas."

No stranger to the whims of the military, Percy nodded. "What about Hannah? Did you get your head out of your ass? Because that girl is the best thing to ever happen to you."

An arm slipped around his waist and a grinning Hannah confirmed, "He did. And yes, I am."

Who was he to argue with the truth? Ryan pulled her close, wanting to keep her by his side as long as absolutely possible, needing to memorize the imprint of her body pressed against his to carry with him on the long, hard road ahead.

"You're good?" Percy asked, taking in the embrace.

He pressed a kiss to her brow. "We're good."

Nodding in satisfaction, Percy pushed to his feet and socked him in the arm. "I told you you needed a woman."

"Percy—"

"What's this about a woman?" Trisha came into the den, a kitchen towel in her hands. As she took in Ryan's arm around Hannah, she clutched it to her mouth, her eyes going suspiciously shiny. "Oh!"

Busted. "Mom, don't you dare cry."

"Oh, shut up. I'm allowed to be happy my son's happy."

He braced himself for…well, he didn't know what. He wouldn't put it past his mother to have a preacher on speed dial.

Hannah squeezed him and lifted her mouth to his ear. "Don't worry. I give good Mom." She stepped toward Trisha, hand outstretched. "In all the crazy, I don't think we really had the chance to be properly introduced. I'm Hannah Wheeler."

Trisha squeezed her hand. "Trisha Malone, and I am very, very glad to meet you." Raising her voice, she hollered, "Mike! Boys! Come meet Ryan's new girlfriend."

He opened his mouth to say...something, expecting Hannah to balk. Instead, those dimples winked on and she followed his mom back into the kitchen.

"That," Percy observed, "is one helluva woman."

"Yes. Yes she is." He wished, more than anything, that they had more time. That he hadn't wasted any with his head up his ass. But even that wouldn't have been enough. And now he had to share his last hours with Hannah with the rest of his family, who he'd shortchanged on this trip stateside. It seemed there was never enough time. Robbie was proof enough that there was never a guarantee of getting more than the moment you were in. That just made him want to cling to this one, to these last hours with Hannah, with his family, all the more.

When Trisha announced it was nearly time to eat, Ryan helped Percy with the new routine of checking his blood sugar and taking his insulin. Then they joined the others at the dining room table that Hannah had somehow transformed into a wonderland in the past ten minutes. He took a moment to appreciate that, to appreciate her as they took their seats and his mother said grace. As Hannah's hand snaked over to twine with his beneath the table, he decided there was a helluva lot to be thankful for this holiday season.

Dinner was a raucous affair of food and laughter and shared memories. Hannah, predictably, charmed his entire family. She rolled with all of it, as if she'd been joking with his brothers and teasing his dad for years. Trisha grew more smitten by the minute, already issuing invitations to future family events that he might not even be home for. Before she could start on the guest list for a wedding or name their future dog, he shoved back from the table.

"Sadly, I have to go."

His family, well-versed in this routine, rose along with him. He already had his bag packed and loaded in Smitty's truck, so there was nothing left but to say his goodbyes. He accepted back-thumping hugs from his dad and brothers. Percy added a knuckle-cracking squeeze of a handshake. Then his mother shoved a care package of leftovers into his hands. "For when you get hungry on the road."

Given the weight of the container, she was convinced he'd starve to death on the six-hour drive. But he took the box and gave her a tight squeeze. "I'm sorry I didn't get to see much of you on this trip."

"Next time." It was an order.

"Yes ma'am."

They all drew back to the porch, giving him a little questionable privacy with Hannah. She followed him down to the truck, waiting as he put the leftovers in the cab. When he reached for her, she flowed into his arms with no hesitation.

He didn't ask again if she was sure. He didn't try to convince her that he was a bad bet or that she deserved better. He just held on, confident that over the coming months, she'd do the same. That they'd get that chance for more. He was trying her optimism on for once. It wasn't familiar, but he found it sat on him a lot more comfortably with her pressed against him.

"I'll be back. I don't know when, don't know how, but I'm gonna be back."

"I know," she whispered.

He pulled back enough to look into her face, skimming his fingers through that long, silky hair. "And in the meantime, you're going to do amazing things and kick ass and tell me all about it." It would have to be enough. For now.

"Speaking of…I heard back about my application to the small business incubator."

"When?" How had she not told him about this?

"A few days ago."

Translation: When we were fighting.

Well, nothing to be done about that now. "And?"

She shrugged and offered a sheepish smile. "I got in."

"That's fantastic!" He scooped her into a twirling hug. "You're gonna be awesome."

"Yeah, I am." She squeezed him tight. "I'm going to miss you."

He ached at how long it would be before he saw her again, touched her again. "We'll talk and write. I'll call whenever I can." It was a promise to himself as much as her.

She pulled something out of her coat pocket. "With everything going on, I didn't get you a Christmas present."

"You are my Christmas present."

"Flatterer." She bumped his shoulder with a grin, but he didn't miss the extra shine to her eyes. "Anyway, I did get you this, to take back with you."

He opened the envelope, sliding out the contents. It was a single photograph of the two of them at the dance out at Applewhite Farms, looking at each other rather than the camera. They hovered on the brink of a kiss, standing right below one of the clusters of mistletoe. It immediately took him back to the feel of her in his arms, the warmth in her eyes, and the way the world had faded away to nothing but her in that single, perfect moment.

"Tara took it. She thought we might want copies. I've got one, too."

The thickness in his throat took a moment to swallow. "It's perfect." He lifted his gaze to her. "You're perfect."

"Perfect for you anyway."

"Definitely that." Drawing her in, he kissed her, long and slow. Lingering, to memorize everything about this moment. When his brothers began to hoot from the porch, he shot up one middle finger and didn't stop what he was doing until he knew he was pushing the envelope with time. Only then did he ease back, pressing his brow to hers. "I have to go."

"I know. Call me when you get there?"

"It'll be late."

"I don't care. Hearing your voice will be worth a little lost sleep."

He let her go, reluctance in every move as he climbed into the truck. The engine grumbled to life, and he rolled down the window for one last touch of her hand.

"I'll be seeing you, Elf Girl."

The dimples winked on as she squeezed his hand. "I'm counting on it, Sergeant."

They didn't say goodbye.

He kissed her knuckles, lifted his hand in a wave to his family, and backed out of the drive. She followed the truck so that the last thing he saw in his rearview mirror was her standing in the middle of the street, her hair whipping in the winter wind, color high in her cheeks as she waved until he was was out of sight.

He was gonna move mountains to get back to that woman.

EPILOGUE

ONE YEAR LATER

"Since we can't get the mini topiaries, we'll need to come up with some other centerpiece for the table arrangements. With the wedding being in a week, we're getting short on time." Whitney Edmonds, the divorcée who'd opened an event planning business down the hall from Hannah several months back, was more than a little rattled. Her usually perfectly coifed blonde hair was piled in a messy bun, chunks escaping at odd intervals, as if she'd started to run her hands through in frustration and caught her fingers. "I don't know *why* anybody wants to get married so close to Christmas."

Relieved at the interruption to her own thoughts, Hannah rose from her desk. "It'll be fine. Let's go brainstorm."

When she'd started at the small business in-cubator nearly a year before, she'd been over-whelmed at everything involved with opening her own firm. While her Christmas decorating efforts had helped to get the word out about her services, building a sustainable client list that would actually make for a living wage had been harder than she imagined. Not until Whitney had arrived and ended up needing help with her first full wedding did everything click into place. Hannah enjoyed the mix of challenges from more traditional interior de-sign jobs to shorter-term event decor, and she'd gotten a new best friend in the bargain.

With the business growing steadily, she'd finally moved into her own place. She still spent a lot of time with Carolanne, but she didn't miss her sister's baker's hours. And it was nice to have total privacy for her phone calls and video chats with Ryan. They'd kept in touch as well as they could, availing themselves of every possible form of long-distance communication. Since Christmas, she'd managed to see him in Washington, D.C. for thirty-six hours over the summer, but he hadn't been back in the U.S. since. It wasn't enough. She missed him like a limb, worried about him during the long stretches he was on mission and incommunicado. But someday—someday he wouldn't be at the whim of the U.S. government. That day would not be this holiday season. He wasn't even getting to come home this Christmas.

It would be fine. They'd celebrate whenever he managed to get leave again. Her parents had hit town a couple of hours ago, and she just needed to wrap work for the day before heading over to Carolanne's for a family dinner. With them staying the next several days for the holiday, there was plenty to focus on right here in Wishful.

Retreating to the conference room, Hannah

and Whitney began listing out options, making note of what materials they had readily available and what could be overnighted via the internet. That sent Hannah's distracted brain down a rabbit hole, trying to remember if she'd finished her Christmas wrapping so she could take the gifts over tonight. From there, she took a mental trip through the massive care package she'd shipped to Ryan, wondering when it would get there and if he and his team would like the decorations she'd sent. Would it help cheer them up or just make them homesick? She was banking on the former, but it was her first major holiday as a military girlfriend. Maybe she should've asked first.

"Earth to Hannah. What do you think of those blown-glass ornaments we looked at by that artist in Eden's Ridge? We could incorporate them on mini Christmas trees maybe."

"What?" She blinked, zeroing in on Whitney's expectant face. "Oh, sorry. My focus is shot." She needed to get it together so they could put the finishing touches on this winter wedding for Wynne Montgomery.

Whitney smirked. "Perhaps your attention would be held better by a certain bearded hottie in uniform?"

A pang echoed through her heart. *If only.* "That would definitely catch my attention."

"Good to know."

At the deep, resonant voice, she whirled.

Ryan stood in the doorway of the conference room in his BDUs, bag slung over his shoulder, exhaustion etched around his eyes, a smile on his face.

She was running, leaping into his arms almost before he could drop his bag. "You're here. You're here." She peppered kisses over his face, her arms and legs tightening around him as he staggered a little beneath her onslaught. "How are you here? Never mind. That can wait for a minute."

Her mouth fused to his. He took a couple of steps, turning until her back was to a wall and he had better leverage. Then he pulled back for a moment, cupping her face in his hands and lowering his lips to hers in a deep, toe-curling, panty-melting kiss that went a long damned way to making up for the time and distance apart.

Dimly, she heard Whitney muttering, "I'm just gonna give y'all some privacy." Then the door to the conference room closed.

When they finally broke apart, breathless, Hannah couldn't release him. He was *here.* "Oh my God, I missed you so much."

"I missed you, too."

She pulled back far enough to see his face. "How are you here? You said you couldn't come home for Christmas."

He let her slide down his body, but his hands gripped her hips, kneading a little, as if he couldn't quite let her go either. "I pulled a few strings. I had to give you your Christmas present in person."

"I don't want anything but you."

Amusement and heat lit his eyes as a grin curved his lips. "I think you'll want this."

Her heart went slow and thick in her chest as he turned away and dug in one of the pockets of the bag. Was he…?

He pulled out a fat envelope and passed it over. "Open it."

The back flap wasn't sealed. She slid the contents out and unfolded the pile, finding a bunch of paperwork with official-looking seals from the United States Army. "What am I looking at?"

"I should probably have put the last page on the front. It ought to make more sense."

Shuffling the pages, she found a letter from the University of Mississippi Medical School.

Dear Mr. Malone,

We are pleased to offer you a position in our incoming class for the coming fall semester—

Her head snapped up. "This is an acceptance into medical school."

His grin turned smug. "It is."

"Which makes all the rest of this—?"

"My paperwork to separate from the Army.

I'm not gonna re-up. I'm coming home for good."

I'm coming home. His words echoed through her head, pinging around until they settled in her heart, warming it like a coal. "Really?"

"Really."

"Ryan," she whispered. Then she was in his arms again, her mouth on his, the papers squashed between them. He was coming home.

Some time later, when they'd surfaced to breathe, she demanded, "How long have you been sitting on this?"

"I started working on it right after I left you last Christmas." He combed his fingers through her hair in that way he had and smiled at her. "I told you, you made me want something else."

She hadn't known he'd been ready to change everything. He hadn't said a word. "Why didn't you tell me?"

On a shrug, he dropped into a chair, tugging her into his lap. "What if you changed your mind about me? About us?"

"Ryan Malone, that is not gonna happen."

"I don't know," he drawled. "You might get sick of seeing me all the time."

"That's going to take a very, very long time. And I'd like to see more of you in very short order."

Grinning, he tipped his face up to hers. "I support this plan. How far to your new place? You can give me the naked tour and then you can see as much of me as you want for the next —oh—forty-eight hours or so."

Her body went molten at the idea of two whole uninterrupted days with him. And then reality knocked her over the head. "That sounds —amazing. But there's just one thing we have to do first."

"Stop for condoms? I've got that covered."

She snorted a laugh. "Look at you, being all Mr. Boy Scout. But no. I wasn't expecting you and…well, my parents are in town for Christmas."

His face blanked. "They're staying with you?"

"No. With Carolanne. But I'm expected at

family dinner in a couple of hours. Since you're actually in town…you could come meet them."

"Meet your parents," he repeated.

Was her badass, Delta Force boyfriend actually…nervous?

"It'll be fine. They're going to love you—because I do." She hadn't told him in all these months. She'd wanted to be able to touch him, to see him when she did.

His chestnut eyes darkened, and he reached up to cup her cheek. "I love you, too, Hannah Wheeler."

She bowed her head, pressing her brow to his as the warmth of joy spread through her, rich and intoxicating as mulled wine.

"You said we had a couple hours before dinner?"

"Yeah."

Plucking her out of his lap, he set her on her feet and grabbed her hand. "Then we have enough time to get back to your place so I can show you exactly how much."

She was still laughing as he dragged her from the building.

~

Choose Your Next Romance!

Next up in the Wishful lineup is a delightful friends-to-lovers romance set against a class reunion. If you've got high school or prom trauma, you're gonna love *Dancing Away With My Heart*. Plus, you'll get to see Jace and Tara's (*Dance Me A Dream*) wedding!

If you're in the mood for more friends-to-lovers, you can check out my latest Wishful Meet Cute Romance, *Once Upon A Rescue*. This one features a Mississippi blizzard, an adorkable firefighter, and a boatload of dogs. And, of course, the Casserole Patrol!

OTHER BOOKS BY KAIT NOLAN

A complete and up-to-date list of all my books can be found at https://kaitnolan.com.

THE MISFIT INN SERIES
SMALL TOWN FAMILY ROMANCE

- *When You Got A Good Thing* (Kennedy and Xander)
- *Til There Was You* (Misty and Denver)

- *Those Sweet Words* (Pru and Flynn)
- *Stay A Little Longer* (Athena and Logan)
- *Bring It On Home* (Maggie and Porter)

RESCUE MY HEART SERIES
SMALL TOWN MILITARY ROMANCE

- *Baby It's Cold Outside* (Ivy and Harrison)
- *What I Like About You* (Laurel and Sebastian)
- *Bad Case of Loving You* (Paisley and Ty prequel)
- *Made For Loving You* (Paisley and Ty)

MEN OF THE MISFIT INN
SMALL TOWN SOUTHERN ROMANCE

- *Let It Be Me* (Emerson and Caleb)
- *Our Kind of Love* (Abbey and Kyle)

WISHFUL SERIES

SMALL TOWN SOUTHERN ROMANCE

- *Once Upon A Coffee* (Avery and Dillon)
- *To Get Me To You* (Cam and Norah)
- *Know Me Well* (Liam and Riley)
- *Be Careful, It's My Heart* (Brody and Tyler)
- *Just For This Moment* (Myles and Piper)
- *Wish I Might* (Reed and Cecily)
- *Turn My World Around* (Tucker and Corinne)
- *Dance Me A Dream* (Jace and Tara)
- *See You Again* (Trey and Sandy)
- *The Christmas Fountain* (Chad and Mary Alice)
- *You Were Meant For Me* (Mitch and Tess)
- *A Lot Like Christmas* (Ryan and Hannah)
- *Dancing Away With My Heart* (Zach and Lexi)

WISHING FOR A HERO SERIES (A WISHFUL SPINOFF SERIES)
SMALL TOWN ROMANTIC SUSPENSE

- *Make You Feel My Love* (Judd and Autumn)
- *Watch Over Me* (Nash and Rowan)
- *Can't Take My Eyes Off You* (Ethan and Miranda)
- *Burn For You* (Sean and Delaney)

MEET CUTE ROMANCE
SMALL TOWN SHORT ROMANCE

- *Once Upon A Snow Day*
- *Once Upon A New Year's Eve*
- *Once Upon An Heirloom*
- *Once Upon A Coffee*
- *Once Upon A Campfire*
- *Once Upon A Rescue*

SUMMER CAMP
CONTEMPORARY ROMANCE

- *Once Upon A Campfire*
- *Second Chance Summer*

ABOUT KAIT

Kait is a Mississippi native, who often swears like a sailor, calls everyone sugar, honey, or darlin', and can wield a bless your heart like a saber or a Snuggie, depending on requirements.

You can find more information on this

RITA ® Award-winning author and her books on her website http://kaitnolan.com. While you're there, sign up for her newsletter so you don't miss out on news about new releases: https://kaitnolan.com/newsletter/